CANDLELIGHT GEORGIAN SPECIAL

CANDLELIGHT REGENCIES

A BOND OF HONOUR

Joan Vincent

A CANDLELIGHT
GEORGIAN SPECIAL

Published by
Dell Publishing Co., Inc.
1 Dag Hammarskjold Plaza
New York, New York 10017

Dell ® TM 681510, Dell Publishing Co., Inc.

ISBN: 0-440-10858-6

Printed in the United States of America

First printing—August 1980

To "the Trees"
and
ma bonne amie Barbe

A BOND
OF HONOUR

1

It snowed. Snow, in fact, seemed to the travelers the beginning and the end. For a time it had blotted out everything; nothing existed but the whiteness, the frigidity.

As the snow deepened on the road and thickened in the sky, the postilion began to have a care for his horses. It had taken a generous glint of the realm's coin to convince him to undertake the journey, for the clouds had hung low and full.

He would have been quit of them yesterday if the lady had been able to hire a substitute, but none was available despite her liberal offers. He had not the heart to refuse her with the wee ones clinging to her. A base man must be hers for husband, to have to travel with just an abigail. Besides, the thought of the fat purse at the end blurred his doubts as to the wisdom of continuing into the regions of Northamptonshire which he had never traveled.

Shortly after midday he pulled his plodding team to a halt. The unexpectedness of it nearly unseated the lady and her abigail and brought forth a new burst of crying from the babe.

Knowing the postilion would not leave his team, Lady Juliane Perrill handed the babe to Cora and, pulling her cloak more firmly about her, stepped out. She sunk to mid-calf as she came off the last step but the only notice she gave was to raise her skirts as she tramped tiredly to the postilion's side.

"What is it now?"

"The horses must rest—the snow is becoming too deep. 'Haps we might turn and go back toward sure lodgings?"

"That would be foolishness—we could not reach there by nightfall, which it almost is like now with this snowfall. I am certain we shall find an inn a short distance hence. Proceed as soon as the team has rested. It would be unwise to let them stand still for too long," she ended knowledgeably.

As if accustomed to instant obedience, she turned and plodded back to the coach. A spark of admiration for her stirred in the postilion, but did not ease his worry.

Back inside the coach, Lady Juliane took the babe and proceeded to quiet her.

"How much farther is it, Aunt Juliane?" a small voice piped from a mound of fur beside Cora.

"Not far, André, but remember, you are to call me 'Mama' for now. Are you warm enough?" she asked, anxiety creeping into her voice.

"Yes . . . Mama. Do I have to sit on these bony bricks? They have no warmth left in them."

10

She nodded for Cora to remove them, sighing. All of the warming bricks had long since lost any comfort. She shivered. Warmth, it seemed, was most difficult to find in England.

"Miss . . ." a stern warning was flashed at Cora, "I mean, my lady, hadn't we be better off to give this up? What good will come of all of us freezing to death? It is useless to go on."

Pursed lips and a fierce dismissing nod were the only reply. Cora sighed inwardly and drew young Master André Renoit de La Croix closer to her for warmth.

Lady Juliane closed her eyes as she hugged the once again sleeping babe closer. She did not fear them freezing—far worse could happen—but she was concerned for the health of the children. André, at the young age of six, had been sturdy enough in their travels but the babe, Leora, was only nine and ten months and a far greater worry. The danger of either of them taking a chill was magnified dreadfully by the weather they had traveled through since leaving the children's home in Rouen.

The erratic forces of chance on life are always surprising, she thought.

When she had left her brother and his wife in India to travel to Rouen, she had resigned herself to the role of spinster aunt which she felt was what lay ahead of her as the years progressed. At her sister's home she would be expected to care for the children in many ways and to be a companion to Judith.

Her father had left a small competence that was not substantial enough for her to set up her own establishment, let alone hire a companion. Her brother

11

and sister would not hear of her taking a paid position as governess or companion. Thus, for the five years since her father's death, she had acted as her widowed brother's hostess, Lord Perrill deciding to stay on in India with his regiment rather than return to the small, crumbling estate of Trewallen left him by his father. She had enjoyed life in India, free for the most part to do as she pleased; she had traveled with him as his duties took him from post to post.

Fascinated, she had watched him succumb to the snares and wiles of Lady Lowen, a recent widow herself just out of mourning, realizing too late what trend the alteration of her position would be after the marriage. Her brother and his new wife graciously plied her with invitations to remain with them but were hard put to feign sadness at her decision to visit Judith for a time.

Correspondence with Judith was erratic at best and, although no reply was received from Juliane's letter telling of her intent to come, Lord Perrill decided that, because Judith was as flighty as a feather, Juliane should proceed to her despite the lack.

A small fuss was raised when she espoused to travel alone but, as she was five and twenty, and not known to draw male attention, this was permitted. Juliane, herself, had some years before faced her looking glass and acknowledged herself sadly lacking in the feminine traits which attract males. It was not that her brown hair was unattractive; indeed with its hints of auburn it was none the worse by comparison except in its style. Juliana felt it a waste to do anything more than the easiest, hence severest styling, and a maid had never been considered for her.

Her spice-brown eyes, with their sparkling vivacity, were her best feature; her complexion had been ruined by her failure to keep covered on her many walking and riding forays. Her lips were full and firm but maintained too stern a line to invite attendance.

She considered herself a large woman, being several inches above the average in height with neither the undernourished-looking thinness nor the tight-laced shape of other beauties. She carried herself gracefully, although it was with grace more manly than feminine. Managing everything she undertook with a calm competence, she caused the women to jealously deride her in gossip and the men to maintain a posture of polite respect. The aloofness with which she responded to the latter assured no advances from an admiring male.

The voyage from Bombay to Portsmouth, although long, had not proven arduous to her. The matter of arranging transportation from Portsmouth to Le Havre and then by land to Rouen had been taken care of by her brother as Earl of Lewallen, his feeling being that such matters were of too complicated a nature to be dealt with by the feminine gender. Although glad to be free from dealing with strangers, Juliane was elated to be free from the tyranny of this prejudice. It had often made matters difficult for her in the past.

A shadow was cast over her enjoyment of her travels by the rumours, which lightly whispered at Portsmouth, became low rumbles of warning as she neared Rouen. The servants and postilions at Le Havre bordered on the insolent, and it was rumoured that the king and his family's confinement would end most unpleasantly for them. The early months of 1793 did not bode well for many and, although Lady Juliane was not ignorant of the cross currents sweeping France, none of her knowledge prepared her for the scene that greeted her at Rouen.

Baron La Croix's small estate lay outside the city and, coming close to it, Lady Juliane saw increasing signs of ill care and disrepair. As the post chaise drew through the gateway and up the path to the door, there were ever-increasing evidences of violence—recent violence. She bade the postilion to await her and with a brave set of the shoulders entered the house. No servants greeted her and the halls and rooms she went through had been terribly mauled. Proceeding to the second floor, she found it was in much the same state. With trembling spirits she continued to the nursery on the third floor. It too had been ravaged.

As she turned to leave the nursery, she heard a stifled whisper and then the sound of leather on wood as if someone shuffled a step. Standing absolutely still, she looked about. Perceiving the doors of the wardrobe were noticeably closed in the disarray of the room, she strode to them without a thought to danger and jerked them open.

Who was the most shocked—Lady Juliane or the young woman who stared at her, wild-eyed—one would have been hard to determine. Both were as statues until a childish voice brought them to the present.

"Cora, you are standing on my foot," said the voice indignantly. "Why must we hide here—you said *mon père* would come for us soon." Tousled gold curls

14

popped into Juliane's view. "Who are you? Did *mon père* send you?"

"No, your papa did not send me but surely he taught his children that they must not speak unless spoken to."

The small face assumed an abashed hue but the eyes belied it.

Lady Juliane reached into the wardrobe and lifted the small boy out. Cora stooped to pick up a bundle which lay further back. Handing it to Juliane, she edged herself out and to the floor.

"Cora, what has happened here? Where is Judith? Are there none here but you?"

"Oh, miss, I mean Lady Juliane, I never thought to see you again." Her voice trembled and tears came to the brink. "You just wouldn't believe what we've been through. God be thanked the children did not see it—oh, it was terrible!" These words were followed by a profusion of tears and wailing. Lady Juliane knew she would learn little until she quieted Cora.

She shook her head in wonder that it was Cora she would find with the children. Judith had insisted on bringing Cora with her as lady's maid when she married and went to live in France. One was as feather-brained as the other and Cora was regarded a sad choice, being much the same age as the younger Juliane.

How had she come to be alone with the children?

Cora was babbling again, but unintelligibly, and Lady Juliane would have wrung her hands in despair but for the babe in them. Looking about for a safe place to bestow her, she felt a tug on her skirt. Look-

15

ing down and around, she encountered a very serious young face.

"I can tell you what happened."

Turning from Cora and leading him out of the room, Juliane knelt before him and studied him earnestly. For one so young, he was mature far beyond his years. "I am your aunt, Juliane—your mama's sister. I have come from India."

He nodded, which she took to mean acceptance.

"What did happen here, André?"

The small face hardened—reminding Juliane distastefully of his father. "It was only a day or two ago—I forget, when they came. No one tried to stop them." Contempt thickened his young voice. "They ran through the house, yelling, *'liberté!'* and destroying everything. Then I saw them shouting at *ma mère* and she sent Cora to get old Gurie and take us," he pointed at the babe, "away. We hid till all were gone."

Cora had brought her sobbing under control and, as she lumbered into the hall, Juliane looked to her to finish the tale.

"They were not even peasants from our estate, my lady, but ruffians and all manner. They said the king was dead; that the baron's wealth was to be theirs. Madame La Croix tried to stop them and they . . ." she sobbed anew, throwing her hands up to cover her reddened, swollen face.

André took Juliane's hand firmly in his and tugged. She followed reluctantly; a sense of what he wanted to show her hovered close.

They came out through the double doors that opened onto a veranda at the rear of the house over-

16

looking the gardens. Leading her down the steps, he went only a short distance further and stopped before a massive rose bed. In the center was a fresh mound of earth.

"Cora says Mama will never wake up—*Est-ce la vérité?*"

Juliane looked from the stark mound to the questioning eyes of the boy-child.

She knelt and drew him close with her free arm. "No, André, your mama will not wake again." A tear rolled down her cheek; memories of their childhood danced before her. Judith, ever gay and carefree, laughing and dancing through life, did not belong there.

André pulled back and raised his small hand to brush her tears away.

"Why are you sad? Cora says Mama will be happy forever in heaven—dancing and going to parties like she loved."

Juliane buried her grief. "Yes, yes she will." She rose, and they walked hand in hand back to the veranda where Cora stood waiting.

"I am sorry she had to be buried there, my lady, but it was the only place we were able to dig . . ." she faltered.

Juliane cut her off with an understanding nod and handed Leora to her. "When do you expect Baron La Croix to return?"

Anger and terror flamed afresh on Cora's features. "They say he knew they were coming and left us, so he could escape them," she spat out. "How true it is I can't say, but he left hurriedly the morning before they came and with no word when to expect his return. Madame La Croix was very upset."

Juliane did not know her brother-in-law well, but she had never liked him. Her vague prejudice led her to believe what Cora said was true.

Back in the main salon, she asked, "What of the other servants? Has no one been here from Rouen?"

"The servants have all deserted us—they believe the revolutionaries will come back—others believe the nonsense about each one getting a piece of the baron's land. The people from the town are struck with fear. What happened here can happen to them. No one will help us."

Juliane did some mental calculations. They all ended at the same point—she must see to the safety of the children. It was doubtful the baron would return. Who could she turn to; where could they go?

Racking her brain, she grasped at a glimmer—her mother's brother, the one they never saw or spoke of—Tedfore, no, Thedfar; no, it was Thedford. She smiled as she recalled the one time he was mentioned just before Judith's marriage. A letter had been received from him for Judith and had thrown her mother into hysterics. It appeared he had never married and as a wedding gift to Judith, was making his will to name her firstborn son as his heir. The sisters had gotten many girlish giggles from this but their parents were tight-lipped and unresponsive to questions, even refusing to allow Judith to reply to the letter.

André would be his heir—she must take the children to him. Even if he had died, there would be a home, a safe haven awaiting them. He was the only close relative she knew of; Lord and Lady Lewallen would not welcome her back with two children while on their honeymoon, or ever, thought Juliane, remembering Lady Edith's dislike of children.

Having seized upon a solution, she was thankful for the full purse Lord Lewallen had insisted she travel with. It would be most useful. She ordered Cora to pack whatever remained of the children's clothing that was undamaged or repairable. They would travel to Northamptonshire. The Thedford land would be known by someone and they had little choice open to them.

Her head snapped back smartly against the unpadded seat of the coach, bringing Lady Juliane quickly to the present. The cold engulfed her.

2

Unknown to Lady Juliane's party, they were not to be alone for long. The road on which they were traveling would shortly converge with another from London, upon which was dangerously speeding a light phaeton drawn by two pairs of highsteppers. The intense blue and white colours of the phaeton were from the crest of the Tretain family. Handling the reins with careless ease was the present holder of the family coronet.

The Earl of Tretain, Lord Adrian, could not be called handsome. Already at one and thirty, his dusky black hair was rife with white. There was a harshness about his features which bespoke mistrust, and his cool grey eyes were usually bored. His indolent manners were belied by the litheness of his tall, spare frame. Those who knew of him termed him a corinthian, a top o' the trees horseman, an out and outer, but, although his reputation was broadly known, he was not.

When in London, he could be found at all the elite soirees and balls, attending the best clubs; but he was there little. For the past five years he had traveled extensively—for what reason no one knew, but then, with his wealth, they said, he did not need a reason.

The Earl of Tretain had but recently returned to London, coming from France, it was rumoured. He was there a week before his presence became known, causing hope to grow in the breasts of those anxious mamas with marriageable daughters. Their hope was brief, for no sooner was his presence known than they learned he had been summoned to Trees, the family estate in Northamptonshire where his mother resided.

Lord Adrian was accustomed to summonses from his mother; he was not accustomed to answering them in person. Not long after he had reached the age of majority, he had concluded that, until he should marry, his mother would make any visit most uncomfortable. He had no desire for the country misses she irreverently put in his way, and she had no use for his taste in women. They had been at a standoff for some time. The factor that decided him on this visit was an accompanying note from her solicitor stating that Lady Tretain was not in good health—a visit might be wise. Knowing his mother, this could be a ruse, but the solicitor was not known to be in his mother's coils. The solicitor had made advance arrangements should he decide to come, so that the best accommodations would be his at all posting inns along the way.

With the suddenness that characterised many of his decisions, Lord Tretain shucked aside all plans and ordered his phaeton and double team, even though the time of year and vagaries of weather did not portend well for traveling in such vehicles.

Mallatt grimaced at his Lord Tretain. He had spent the past ten years with the man and still could not say he understood him. While he shivered and prayed to be spared a broken neck, Tretain reveled in the cold and snow, keeping the teams at a pace few would have dared in the prevailing conditions.

Quite like his lordship, thought Mallatt, who through long service had learned that my lord's usually conservative behaviour could be cast aside on the flick of an eyelash. There had been many incidents over his years of service that made him shake his head. Take the wager over the ducks crossing the road—that was a rare one by the time it ended. Oh well, the gentry were entitled and that certainly included Lord Tretain.

Most believed the earl spent his days leisurely traveling, squandering the money his family had amassed. Mallatt was one of the few that knew the truth and his faith in the man was unshakeable.

Casting a look about, Mallatt thought to bespeak his lord to come to a safer pace, but seeing the relaxed face next to his, a grin erasing the harshness for the first time in many a month, he resigned himself simply to hanging on with the fond hope of preserving life and limb.

Lord Tretain controlled the two teams easily. He felt their every move and was totally absorbed in their flowing movement. For this reason and because he was seated to the right, he did not detect the movement to his left directed squarely in his path, until it was too late.

By the time both he and the postilion from the coach realized the danger, there was no chance to escape the encounter. As skillfully as Lord Tretain tried to maneuver his teams, there was no way to check their forward momentum quickly enough or to swerve them from the path of the other coach. As the postilion's team became entangled between his pairs, Lord Tretain's phaeton lurched wildly. The earl pulled hard on the reins, attempting to control his horses as Mallatt lunged for a hold.

Screams and shouts filled the air as those within the coach were thrown about by the frantic lunging and rearing of the entwined teams. For long seconds the phaeton hung in the air, settled to the ground, and again twisted into the air. Standing to leap down, Lord Tretain was thrown to one side as his teams plunged and thrashed wildly in their traces. The earl realized as he fell that the phaeton was toppling over. Mallatt tumbled free in an awkward sprawl away from the earl and then all was darkness as Tretain's head struck the rising wheel of the overturning phaeton.

3

During the first few seconds following the meeting of the two vehicles, Lady Juliane's comprehension failed her. As she struggled to rise amidst the tangle of petticoats, arms, legs, cloaks, and coverings, her reason reasserted itself. The constant heave-ho action of the coach, which made sorting herself free from the other three bodies on the coach floor nigh impossible, bespoke a mishap of the adverse sort.

Above the caterwaul of Cora, the wail of the babe, and André's shrieks for whomever was atop him to remove himself, she heard angry men's voices and the neighs and struggles of frightened horses.

Outside the coach, the postilion and Mallatt cooled enough in the snowfall to realize that the shouting match they were engaged in would help no one. Each snapped his mouth shut abruptly and turned to unhitch and untangle the teams.

With the coach at a standstill, Lady Juliane was finally able to disengage herself from the tangle. Her rise from the tumbled mass added the sound of rending cloth to the discordant symphony already issuing from the coach.

Without pausing to check the nature of the damage, she yanked and pried Cora from her extraordinary position on the coach floor and back to her seat, thus freeing André to scamper up with as piqued an expression as his youth allowed him to muster.

Juliane examined him and the babe quickly and found them angered and frightened in turn, but unharmed except for a few bruises. As far as she could ascertain, Cora also was unharmed, although babbling that they must turn back.

"Quiet yourself, Cora," she admonished sternly. "We are unhurt. Comfort Leora while I see what caused this and what damage may have been done."

Stepping out of the right-hand side of the coach, she was surprised to see a phaeton on its side; she had had no glimpse of it before. The two men had almost completed the separation of the teams as she trudged through the snow to them.

"Was anyone hurt in the phaeton?" she asked as she came up to the two.

Mallatt threw a startled glance at her, then dropped his work with a "My God, my lord!"

"What is it?" asked Juliane, somewhat startled by this reaction.

"Begging your pardon, but my lord, the Earl of Tretain—he isn't about and I forgot him in the confusion."

Leaving the teams to the postilion, he trudged

around the fallen phaeton. Lifting her skirts to ease her movement, Juliane followed in his path.

As they rounded the back of the phaeton they saw a splash of black stretched out against the snow. It was fast becoming white itself in the continuing snowfall.

Coming closer to the prone figure, Juliane saw the rose-red splotch slowly spreading beneath the head.

Mallatt knelt and tenderly turned the earl onto his back.

"He must have struck his head in the fall. He's breathing still," he added after pushing a hand beneath the greatcoat to the chest.

"I will get something to bind the wound—check for broken bones while I do," Lady Juliane commanded.

The care he held for his lord pressed Mallat to obedience, riled though he was by orders from someone other than the earl. He finished as Lady Juliane returned.

She knelt at the earl's side, folding a white cloth. "Press this to the wound tightly."

Mallatt did so with a frown; did the woman think him an idiot?

His eyes were diverted from the earl by the screech of ripping cloth. He stared as Lady Juliane finished tearing a strip from the bottom of one of her petticoats.

"What is wrong with you? Hold his head up—how am I to bind it if you do not?"

He watched with admiration as she deftly bound Lord Tretain's head wound with skilled ease.

Finished, she observed the earl. Shaking her head,

she said, "It is too bad of me, but I have neither vinaigrette nor smelling salts. Do you . . ."

The disbelieving look convinced her to forego the remainder of the question; evidently the Earl of Tretain was not subject to fainting spells.

"We must get the earl out of the snow as soon as possible. Cover him with this." She reached back for the fur she had dropped before kneeling, "And let us see if my coach has any damage."

Returning to the opposite side, she was taken aback by the sight of the postilion trying to turn his team and coach around to face the direction from which they had traveled.

"What are you doing?" rang clear in the air.

"I be heading back to sure lodging, that's what I be doing. If it is to your mislike, you can stay here," the postilion snorted angrily. "The blunt you promise will do me naught if I lose my means of livelihood gettin' it."

Cora, who had been leaning her head out of the coach to hear, hastened from the coach to add her pleas to the postilion's words.

"Yes, my lady, let us turn back. No good will come of going further—this be a sign for certain!"

Lady Juliane's ire was raised. "Are both of you fools? We have come more than a half-day's journey already. It is idiocy to turn back," she flared out at them.

"Call it what you like—I turn back now." His point settled, the postilion grabbed the bridles of the team and stepped to guide them in the turn.

Lady Juliane stifled further protest, realizing the hopelessness of it. What was she to do? If she went back, she would not have enough money to travel the entire way. As she was pondering, a hand touched her arm.

"Excuse me, my lady," bowed Mallatt. "How far is it to the posting inn the coachman intends to return to?"

"Over a half day's travel—longer with the snow getting worse," she answered bitterly.

"Too far," murmured Mallatt as to himself.

"Yes. I have told him so but he cannot get the notion out of his head. Do you know the lay of the land here?" she asked, a faint hope lifting within her.

Mallatt frowned and rubbed his hands together seeking some warmth, "I have not come this way frequently with my lord, and seldom do we stop when we travel this way, but reason says an inn or some shelter must lie ahead. I think I recall some sort of buildings we pass going this way."

"Perhaps you could persuade him to change his mind."

"I doubt it—hirelings of his sort, you know, have little pride."

"What will you do?"

"Heave my lord atop a horse and make for warmth."

Lady Juliane surveyed the two pair and the postilion who had almost completed turning his coach. "Could we come with you?"

Mallatt looked at her askance. "Meaning no disrespect, my lady, but that is impossible."

"Why?" she asked boldly.

"Because there is no coach, no saddles for the cattle, no . . . it is out of the question!"

"I think not. André can ride the horse with the lame foot—you must ride with the earl to keep him on—that leaves one for my maid and myself and one for the necessary baggage," she finished decisively.

"My lady, I am certain my lord Tretain would not approve."

"He is not able to approve or disapprove."

"My lady," pleaded Cora. "Do not do this—it is . . . would be most unseemly—there is no way to ride. They are such huge beasts. You cannot mean to do it."

"Of course I mean to do it. We have little choice. Do not be missish about this."

"I will not go," bawled Cora, causing Leora to squirm and cry once more.

Juliane took Leora. Her body aching from cold and fatigue, she was rapidly tiring of Cora's constant tears and fretting. "Then return with the postilion!" She handed Leora to a startled Mallatt and strode to the coach. Calling on André, she asked him to hand out her reticule, then reached up and lifted him down. From her reticule she pulled out some coins. Tramping up to the postilion, she slapped some in his hand; the remainder she handed to Cora.

Taking Leora back from Mallatt, she ordered, "Remove our baggage from the coach."

"My lady, I cannot. Without your maid it is even more disastrous to attempt coming with us."

"Do as I say, or I will." She stepped forward and started to hand Leora back to him once again.

Muttering under his breath, Mallatt stepped back and bumped into André.

"Why don't you do as *ma mère* tells you?" asked André.

Mallatt looked from the small lad to the defiant Juliane. Twisting his face into an expression of resignation and displeasure, he surrendered and went to the coach to remove the luggage.

Blubbering, Cora caught at her cloak. "My lady, don't do this—you must come with us!"

Lady Juliane looked down at her icily, saying nothing.

"What happens you bring on yourself," Cora flung over her shoulder as she rushed back to the coach, lest she be left behind. She had done more than her duty in warning Lady Juliane, she assured herself.

The postilion urged his team off even as Mallatt clambered down with the last bag. He stood watching it out of sight, then shook himself and went about placing Lady Juliane's and the children's baggage beside the overturned phaeton.

Before he finished this, Lady Juliane joined him. She sorted out two valises. Opening one of her larger bags, she withdrew necessities for herself and added those to the contents of the children's valises. The remainder she bid Mallatt to place under the phaeton for protection from the weather.

This bid was followed by the command to ready a bag for the earl and himself and to get the baggage secured to one of the horses.

Mallatt had begun to seethe under this flurry of orders, thinking it impudent of her to assume authority. She was above him in station, but a woman nonetheless, and should have collapsed into hysterics long ago. Her control was not proper in the least, he decided; but stealing looks at her while doing as she bid, he softened toward her. She was younger than he had first imagined, and her bearing and manner bespoke the best of the gentility. She had, after all, been addressed as "my lady" by the blubbering female of a maid. There was also an obvious sense of fatigue about her, an air of strain, and he could not but admire that despite this she seemed to have not a thought for herself, but patiently attended to the children and the earl while she waited for him to finish.

Baggage secured, he paused, uncertain as how to best get everyone mounted. Gazing at the prone figure of the earl with the children huddled against him and Lady Juliane beside him, he was struck by the image of his lord as a family man. The idea startled him so he shook himself; the earl would not be pleased by such a thought, although Mallatt himself privately thought a family was just what he needed.

Juliane glanced up and perceived the uncertainty in Mallatt's face along with something else, but she was too tired to pursue what it was. Rising, she approached him.

"Before we continue, I feel we should 'properly' introduce ourselves. I cannot address you if I do not know your name," she blushed, hoping he would not mistake her for a snob.

"Indeed, my lady. As I mentioned earlier, yon gentleman is the Earl of Tretain, Lord Adrian. I am Mallatt, his valet."

"I am Lady Juliane—that is Master André and Miss Leora." She opened her mouth as if to add something, then hesitated, biting her lower lip, and with a slight shrug continued, "I had better help you get Lord Tretain astride first."

If Mallatt had noticed she had not given her family name, it was not discernible. Her final statement shocked him. "No, my lady," he disagreed. "I will mount you and the children first."

"No." Lady Juliane clearly wore the look of one accustomed to being obeyed.

Mallatt shrugged inwardly. Let her have her way—his would be the way in the end regardless. "Yes, my lady," he said, bowing.

Together they lifted, shoved, pushed, and pulled Lord Tretain astride—no easy task considering his size and solidity. Adding to the difficulty was the steed's constant shifting, unaccustomed as he was to the commotion and the condition of the rider. Both Juliane and Mallatt were panting by the time they had the earl settled on the horse. He had remained unconscious throughout, much to his benefit.

"Master André," Mallatt called, "are you frightened of horses?"

"*Non.* I have ridden often with *ma mère* and *mon père* at home."

"Come, hold the horse then, stroke him," he said as he led the mount beside one of the upturned wheels. "You, my lady, must hold the earl in place while I get in position behind him."

Juliane was glad of her height and strength as she held the earl's arm while Mallatt scrambled up the carriage front and atop the wheel. It threatened to turn as he stepped across it, but he was able to plop aboard the startled horse before the wheel did so.

"Excellent, Master André. You must be an excellent horseman," praised Mallatt as Lady Juliane took the reins from André and handed them to him.

As he prepared to give his best "now what?" grimace to Lady Juliane, she turned her back and untied the horse with the baggage and the lame one. Leading them up to him, she handed over the reins without even pausing to look at him. Picking up André, she lifted him atop the lame horse.

Mallatt was sure she would now be at an impasse, for how could she mount without a saddle of any sort, let alone with the babe to handle.

Juliane, however, was oblivious to the fact that she should be at loggerheads as to what to do. She merely looked about and decided on a course of action.

Picking up Leora, she placed her atop the up-turned wheel that Mallatt had used to mount. She handed the fur piece to Mallatt to use on the earl. One of the other coverings she bound around André, tucking it under the harness as best she could; the other she laid alongside Leora.

Satisfied that everything was taken care of, she went to the phaeton and pulled out a small trunk. Untying the reins of the last horse, she stepped upon the trunk. She turned to look at Mallatt, who was watching this procedure with intense interest. "Would you be so good as to close your eyes?" she asked.

Mallatt struggled valiantly, if somewhat ineffectively, to suppress a broad grin and did as she asked.

Juliane turned back to the horse and, lifting her skirt and petticoats waist high, flung herself over the horse. With a struggle she squirmed about until she got her leg over and swung up. After endeavouring unavailingly for a few minutes to lower her petticoats and skirt to a modest level, she laughed.

The sound popped Mallatt's eyes open. He looked admiringly at the trim, hosed ankle and calf that was exposed.

"In truth, Mallatt," she tossed at him, "I do not know whether to blush for want of modesty or to curse for want of warmth."

He laughed in reply. "Since you will evidently have to suffer from both, I suggest we get on."

She urged her mount alongside the wheel and snatched Leora and the cover. Bundling the babe as best she could, Lady Juliane settled Leora in the crook of one arm and placed her mount's reins in that hand. Moving alongside Mallatt, she took the reins of André's horse.

"I best lead, my lady. Stay close behind."

An hour later he halted. Lady Juliane came alongside.

"Do you see anything?" she asked through her clacking teeth.

"Only the snow, I fear, my lady. Are you all right?"

Trying to manage her frozen face into a reassuring smile, she nodded.

"Master André, how are you?" asked Mallatt worriedly, as he tried to check the figure of the small boy.

"*Froid,*" came the clear reply.

"Keep your hands covered and hold on tightly. When you think you cannot—call out," he instructed him.

"Do you understand?" shouted Juliane.

"*Oui . . .*'mama.'"

Wordlessly, Mallatt led on.

Juliane lost track of time after that. She felt the arm which cradled Leora grow more numb by the minute. "Will I ever be able to move it again?" she asked herself. Close to exhaustion, she was so very sleepy—even the cold no longer felt so terrible. She was no longer conscious of Mallatt ahead or that her horse was following the first two from instinct, not from her guidance. Juliane fought to retain control, to keep her eyes open—it would be so easy to let them close.

On they plodded through constant, endless white.

4

Lady Juliane snuggled deeper. It was so warm. Her hands and feet tingled painfully but, oh, the warmth!—she had thought never to thaw again. Warm again?

Her eyes opened in alarm. Slowly taking in the surroundings, her alarm grew. The last she could recall was following Mallatt and the dulling awareness of the cold. Evidently, he had found them shelter.

Struggling to sit upright, Lady Juliane saw she was wearing her own nightdress, newly bought at Portsmouth. Why did she not remember getting into it? She surveyed the room once more, ending in locked fascination on the opposite side of the large featherbed.

It could not be? Gingerly, she reached out to touch the pale, beard-stubbled cheek. It was rough to her fingers. She snatched her hand back—what else had she expected?

The face turned toward her—the lids raised, revealing cool grey eyes. She stared down as the lips curled into a smile, making the man more handsome; then the eyes closed once more.

Well, truly, she thought, how dare he smile at me in so intimate a fashion. Not even Lord Dennerly had ever done so and he had "kept company" with her for almost six months. But then, she mentally added, I never did wake up to find myself next to Lord Dennerly.

That thought finally sinking in, she gasped and struggled to throw back the heavy coverlets.

At this moment a large, brisk woman came into the room. Seeing Juliane struggling with the bedding, she came to the bedside and, pushing her back down with one hand, neatly arranged the coverlets with the other, saying, "Now, m'lady, ye will only do yourself harm in trying to be about. Nasty time ye've had of it. Back to sleep with ye."

"But you do not understand," Juliane said agitatedly, striving to rise.

"Oh, ye be worried about the mites," soothed the woman. "They be fine."

"But, I must . . ."

"Ye must rest and regain yer strength. What with a fine man ye 'ave for a husband and the two lovely children. Yer lord will want tending soon enough—he's a lump bigger'n a duck egg on his noggin besides a nasty cut, and I doubt it will put him in good fettle for awhile; ye know what I mean," she winked knowingly.

Juliane just stared at her open-mouthed.

The woman clucked, "Now, I be sorry, m'lady, I be

forgettin' ye gentry ain't so open with yer speakin', ye ladies, I mean."

Juliane found it difficult to make sense of this, but evidently the woman had some misbegotten notion. Perhaps if she could explain. "We had this accident . . ."

"That's what I was tellin' Jove—m' man. But what could bring ye out on a day like it was, is beside me. We couldn't get much from yer man—he was near froze through, as were ye all. But we found yer lord's card, m'lady. T'was only God's blessin' ye didn't lose the children."

Lady Juliane sat up again and started to get out of bed.

"None of that. Ye stay abed till breakfast is ready. The wee maid is sleepin'—had to pry her from yer arm. So 'tis the lad. Ye'll need your strength to cope with 'im," she nodded toward the earl, "or m' name ain't Meg. Nothin' fussier than a pained man. Now stay to bed till I bring ye some porridge—not what yer used to by m' guess, but plenty fillin' and fortifyin'."

Juliane lay back down under the piercing eyes. As Meg disappeared behind the closing door, her thoughts milled turbulently in her mind. She closed her eyes.

This was a dream; it was not happening. I am much too sensible for this. I will open my eyes and find myself in a small chamber at a posting inn with Leora and André, she told herself. Letting out a deep breath, she slowly opened her eyes. It was futile. The earl was still abed with her.

Cautiously, she pried back the many coverlets and stretched her feet to the floor. "Brr." She quickly drew them up before planting them down firmly once more. The cold was not to be escaped.

Spying her wrap lying across the end of the bed, she pulled it on quickly, wrapping the shawl that she found under it around her. Her slippers were at the foot of the bed, and provided relief from the icy floor.

Much better, she thought. Now what to do. "Obviously, Meg thinks we are married, my lord," she spoke softly to the unconscious figure. "To undo that contention would do me more harm than good, at the moment, or ever, unfortunately. If you will remain unconscious, my lord, you will find me a most dutiful wife," she finished, bobbing a deft curtsy.

Turning her back on the bed, she went to warm her hands by the meager fire. What to do? Lord. No sense in being missish about this—must keep my head. Yes. Must find out where we are before I make any decisions.

She looked around. They must have stumbled on a farmer's cottage somehow. This did not have the look of a posting inn—even a modest one—and Meg did not talk as one accustomed to dealing with the "Quality." This must be Meg and . . . this must be their room, she thought, as she took in the meager wardrobe and the scarred but clean washstand.

"Ah, m'lady," Meg growled as she bustled in. "I says to Jove as he was leavin' the house, 'she'll be up and about when I get back', and here ye are. Come, sit here and eat. How ye be feelin'?"

"I am . . . I am fine, truly. I would like to see the children. How is Mallatt?"

"One thing at a time. Ye eat this," she said, sticking

39

the bowl of porridge almost in Juliane's nose. "Then we be gettin' to the others."

Juliane thought if she closed her eyes tight enough, she would have little trouble believing herself to be back in the nursery. No one had ordered her about since that time in her life. She sighed, taking the bowl. Meg was of an age to be her mother, she guessed, kind and motherly looking, despite her rough ways. Right at this moment, Juliane decided, she could use a little mothering.

While Lady Juliane ate, Meg tossed more wood on the fire. "We wouldn't want yer lord any more grumpy than need be," she laughed over her shoulder. "Ye'll be glad to be knowin' the snow has stopped. Me lads think it will be a fine day. In a day or two they'll be able to ferret out yer coach."

Juliane dropped her spoon in surprise—in a day or two? The time element had not occurred to her.

"Now, see," grumbled Meg kindly, "I knew ye be gettin' up too soon." She handed Juliane the spoon, wiping it first on the apron that covered her ample bosom.

"No. I am fine. I must see the children," stuttered Juliane, trying to cover her consternation.

"How be it ye be travelin' without a nurse or nanny and a maid? Yer lord looks plump enough in the pocket for that," questioned Meg.

Juliane couldn't believe she heard herself twitter.

"That is my doing, I am afraid. We are traveling to Lord Tretain's estates and wished for privacy," she blushed. "Besides, there are those at the estate to do those duties," she added as a hurried afterthought.

Enough questions would arise when the phaeton was brought in.

Meg cackled. "I think ye'd be havin' more privacy with a nurse along, but then one never knows."

Juliane had lowered her head over her bowl, eating fiercely to hide her features.

"I'll be back in a moment with yer gown. It needed dryin' and pressin'," Meg smiled from the doorway. "Tsk, tsk," she said to herself as she wagged down the stairs. One would think the girl a newlywed, or perhaps m'lord was too cozy with the nurse. Oh, the gentry. But the girl did seem a good sort, Meg reasoned, concerned about the children and all—not like some we hear of.

Mallatt swung his feet off the narrow cot and looked around.

Ah, yes—he had been placed in with the sons. He shook his head. He could not recall their names nor the farmer's. The night's passings were unrecallable also.

Thank God we stumbled in here—we'd be frozen solid by now. He looked around and spied his clothing neatly folded.

Wonder what they did with Lord Adrian, he mused. Must check on him. And yes, that Lady Juliane and the two children. I'd best be looking in on them all.

The sons' room was on the lower level of the farm cottage, so Mallatt had little trouble finding the kitchen, which seemed to take up most of that floor.

"And good morn to ye," Meg greeted him, as he

41

cautiously entered. "Ye don't look like ye've taken a chill."

"Of course not, my good woman. But I fear Lady Juliane and the wee tykes were not dressed for such an outing. How do they fare?"

"Don't ye go 'good womanin' me—m' name is Meg," she chided him.

"And I am Mallatt," he bowed stiffly. "Lord Adrian's valet."

"A real valet, ye don't say now," chuckled Meg.

"Pardon, ma'am," Mallatt addressed her carefully, "Lady Juliane and the children—are they well? What of my lord? He was injured in the accident."

"Tsk, tsk. I shouldn't keep ye worryin' now, should I? Sit down. A steamin' mug of m' Jove's brew will do wonders for ye."

Mallatt dubiously eyed the concoction that was presently set before him; it was still bubbling. Meg stood before him, hands on hips. "Now ye drink it."

Deciding she outweighed him by several stone, he prudently lifted the mug to his lips and sipped. He swallowed a generous amount, deeming it safe.

"Now, Meg, about . . ."

"Aye, stay in yer breeches. They all be fine. Lady Juliane, ye called her, be as good as new, and the boy child . . ."

"Master André."

"André—that's a foreign-soundin' one. Frog ain't it?" She shrugged aside any forthcoming answer, continuing, "He be fine enough." She shook her head. "Yer lord could well take a fever with that head wound and the cold. The babe, though, be a greater worry." Meg stepped to the cradle beside the fire and

42

bent to draw the covers more firmly about the babe. "She sleeps fitfully and has gotten a cough. I'd say a hard time t'will be hers. What say ye her name be?"

"Mistress Leora."

"Ah, a pretty name for a pretty babe. It be sad she have to take it to the grave so early—but many do this many a day." She clucked her tongue. "Yer master should kno' better'n to gad about with his family in sech weather," she said angrily.

Mallatt choked on his swallow of brew. "Family," he sputtered weakly.

"Him with a fine strong woman and them with two children—he shouldna' take chances with them."

Her back was to the rough table, so Meg did not see the look of puzzlement, consternation, and worry play on Mallatt's features.

Had Lady Juliane given this woman the idea they were all of a party? But no, he was certain she was in no state to talk when they arrived and Lord Adrian certainly—Lord Adrian—

"Has my lord regained consciousness yet?"

"Nay, he be sleepin' like a babe yet. Yer mistress can tell ye more. My Alva just took her gown to her and I reckon she'll be down in a trice to check on the babe—seems that's all she has on her mind."

Mallatt nodded, silent. He was certain Lady Juliane had that on her mind and more. It was her doing for insisting on coming along—things would begin a-popping when his lordship came to his senses and learned the state of affairs. I would hate to be in her place—poor thing, he thought.

What about yourself, his subconscious tweaked him.

Lord Adrian would not look kindly on his handling of matters thus far.

Well, he'd play it mum and see if there wasn't a way to blunder out of this. She mustn't know their thoughts yet, he pondered, or I'd been awakened earlier. Ladies of quality do raise such a fuss at things.

Draining his mug, Mallatt silently commended Meg. She was right, things did look a little better and he certainly felt buoyed. He dug into the steaming porridge she sat before him.

As he finished it, he heard footsteps. Turning, he saw Lady Juliane whose worried face broke into a smile. "Why, Mallatt, how good to see you are unharmed."

He stood and bowed stiffly. "May I say the same to you, my lady."

"André is fine also. I just checked on him, but Alva said Leora was here," she said hesitantly, looking at Meg.

Meg pointed to the cradle.

Juliane hurried to it and knelt. She lay a hand on the babe and threw a startled glance at Meg.

"Aye, m'lady," Meg nodded sadly. "She's taken a chill for sure. I'm readyin' a poultice for her now."

"Hu-umph." Mallatt cleared his throat.

Juliane's gaze swung to him. He could see she was shaken by this news. "I am sorry to bother you, my lady, but how fares Lord Adrian?"

She looked at him blankly.

He came toward her, lowering his voice. "How does my lord do?" he asked again.

A deep blush replaced her blank look; she lowered her eyes.

Oh, they must have said something to her after all, he concluded. Trying to ease her mind, he whispered at her side, "I understand, the, er, 'situation', here. The, uh, conclusion which was drawn. We will find a way out of the toil, never fear." Something prodded him to offer comfort.

Lady Juliane threw him such a grateful look he smiled at her. "That is better. Now, how is Lord Adrian?"

Juliane once more looked to Leora, fiddling with the blankets to hide her blush at the thought of Mallatt learning she and the earl had been bedded together. "He is still unconscious, although he did open his eyes briefly this morning. He does not seem to have taken a fever yet and may regain his senses at any time. One never knows about blows to the head, however. They are unpredictable, his especially with the cold he endured."

Mallatt waited for more. "Anything else, my lady?"

"Yes," she said absentmindedly, vaguely recalling what she would order for her brother. "You should shave Lord Adrian. I feel he would not be pleased to awaken untidy. I left Alva watching him. Take her place. When I can, I will return to the room." The final word spoke dismissal.

Mallatt looked to Meg.

"Top o' the stairs—door to the left. Ye'll find what ye be need'n there I suppose. The bags were placed in that room. Hot water is there." She pointed to the smaller pot hanging over the fire and then to a large bowl on a shelf nearby.

Taking the bowl and dipping it half full, Mallatt proceeded up the stairs. What would he say to Lord

Adrian? How could this be logically explained to raise the fault from his shoulders? His lord was such a stickler at times. One never knew what his reaction would be, and he had never been in a situation quite like this before.

"Not meaning to be disloyal, my lord," he muttered to himself, "but I hope it's a long sleep you have this time."

5

Meg bustled over to the cradle with the poultice. Lady Juliane moved swiftly to the side and watched closely as she skillfully attended to Leora.

"Ye can leave her to me, m'lady—many a sick child I've nursed. If it's possible, we'll have her well in no time a'tal."

Lady Juliane's hands flew as if to quiet her pounding heart; "if possible" echoed in her mind.

Wrapping the babe tightly, Meg stole a look at Juliane. "Here," she said gently, holding out the still bundle. "Ye rock her a spell. The boys will be bringin' milk fresh from the cow soon and we'll see if she'll take some."

Lady Juliane pulled the worn, smoothly polished rocker closer to the warmth of the glowing fire and took Leora gratefully. Smoothing back the corn-silk-fine hair, she rocked, unconsciously humming a nursery tune recalled from the depths of the past. Odd, how attached I have become to the children in such a short time, she thought wistfully. It is as if they are my own.

Musing over Leora, she was startled by tramping feet, blustering voices, and the banging and clattering that accompanied the entry of Jove and his sons.

Jove nodded brusquely at Juliane to acknowledge her presence as he pulled off his warm outer cloak. The larger of the boys shuffled into the center of the room, setting a large pail on the table. "The milk, Ma," he managed to stutter out clumsily, staring all the while at Lady Juliane.

"Well, get out o' them things. The porridge 'tis a waitin'," she cheerfully rebuked them. "And mind yer manners in front o' the Quality."

"Pardon their manners, m'lady," she directed to Lady Juliane, "but we get few visitors here." She took the pail and began to strain the milk into a large crock. "The big'un be Ned and the other'n Jem," she added by way of introductions.

Juliane simply stared at the three, not certain what to say or do. Drawing her wits about her, she said, "It is you we need to thank for saving us. If we had not been given shelter we would all have perished. Thank you sincerely."

"Gosh" and "Gee" were the only replies from the sons.

"Just doin' our Christian duty, ma'am, ah"—Jove's eyes swung to his wife's—"m'lady," he replied gruffly. "Pardon us for eatin' afore ye, but it been a long, cold mornin'."

"Please, feel free to do so," smiled Juliane, becoming a little more at ease.

Alva had entered during this brief exchange and had gone about filling the bowls and setting them on the table before her father and brothers. She was a miniature of her mother, being but five and ten and just beginning to show the same tendency toward plumpness.

Lady Juliane watched the scene with interest. She had never before observed family life other than her own and could recall from her youth none of the warmth and closeness apparent in this group. She felt a pang of envy, but her attention was taken up by a coughing fit from Leora. Failing to quiet it, she became alarmed. Meg was at her side in an instant, forcing some warm, dark liquid between the babe's lips. This caused a terrible pucker and much sputtering, but succeeded in stilling the cough.

Juliane looked at the mug suspiciously.

" 'Tis but home brew, m'lady. It will not harm the wee one and is best for stoppin' the cough."

Juliane nodded worriedly as Meg took Leora.

"Best ye see to yer lord. His man should be finished. Call if ye be needin' anything. I'll take care for the babe—have no worry on that."

Going slowly up the stairs, Juliane worried about Leora's health. It was not until the second series of shrieks for *ma mère* that she became mobilized in their direction. Racing up the last few steps, she flew through the doorway to her right. Swooping to the bed, she scooped up André like a gull plucking fish from the sea. He held on like a leech, his cries slowly subsiding.

"Hush. Hush now. You were having a bad dream. Everything is all right now," Juliane crooned to him, rocking him gently in her arms. Soon he lay still against her, loosening his hold.

She carried him across the hall and tucked him into bed, opposite Lord Tretain's form, which drew a curious glance from Mallatt as well as from André.

"Truly, my lady, do you deem that wise?" he queried as he continued to put his shaving instruments away.

"In my lord's state, it is nothing," she replied carelessly.

"Yes, but we do not know how long this state will last. Have you considered what will happen when he returns to his senses?"

"I imagine he will fly into the boughs, make a dreadful scene of it, and ruin my reputation forever," she answered matter-of-factly. "What else is there? He can like the situation little more than I myself."

Mallatt snapped the valise shut and eyed Lady Juliane carefully. "There is a way, a chance of coming out of this, with a little daring on our part." He scarcely could credit himself with the words. Must be I've been in my lord's service too long—his ways are rubbing off on me, was his startled thought.

"In truth, that would be possible, but only on the chance that Lord Tretain would remain senseless, and it is highly unlikely that he will be so condescending for the two days Meg tells me it will be before they make an effort to fetch the phaeton. When they see it, questions can't help but arise. They will see that it was not made for family travel. I have decided to take what comes—what else is there for me to do?"

Mallatt pondered. This hardly seemed like the

same girl; what had happened to her spirit? Perhaps he had misjudged her after all.

Juliane turned from the fire to face him. There was a hint of an idea in her eye. Beginning tentatively, she studied him. "There is a way out—out of Bedlam, but certainly the end, if it fails, can be no worse than what I now face. Would Lord Adrian hold it against you if you helped in a 'slight' deception?"

Mallatt knew he should resist—that Lord Adrian, indeed, would object—but then Lady Juliane was not at fault in this, and if they could come up to the top, his lordship might eventually agree and even come to see the humour in it. Lord Adrian could not, after all, be the first to throw a stone at a "slight" deception. He smiled broadly.

Lady Juliane flashed a smile in return. "Let us keep the pretense of marriage then. I think we are far enough from civilization here for that to do us little harm, are we not?"

"I believe so, my lady," Mallatt agreed tentatively.

"Then, all we need do is manage these next few days!"

Mallatt raised an eyebrow at this oversimplification, but felt it useless and probably alarming to Lady Juliane to suggest the many difficulties that could occur. Further attention to the matter was deterred as his lordship stirred.

Lady Juliane went to his side, laying a cool hand on his forehead as he twisted beneath the covers. This action caused him to stiffen and remain still, drawing a frown from Juliane.

"Was Lord Tretain in good health before the accident?" she asked Mallatt.

"Yes, my lady. A bit done in perhaps . . ."

She looked to him for further information. He stood, shifting his weight, undecided as to what to tell.

"How does his lordship spend his time?"

"Traveling," answered Mallatt truthfully. "He . . . we, just returned from the continent."

This answer caused Lady Juliane to blanch slightly, but before Mallatt could pursue the cause behind this, the earl's stirrings snared their attention once more.

"What is wrong with him, Mama?" inquired André, who had been watching and listening spellbound to the scene before him. It was enough that he was sharing the bed with the gentleman. Life had certainly become more interesting since *Tante*—Mama— had taken them.

"A fever, André—from being in the snow too long I suppose. You must lie there quietly." Turning to Mallatt she ordered, "Dampen this cloth and return it to me."

Taking the wet cloth, she laid it firmly across Lord Tretain's brow, holding it in place as he tossed his head. "Did you discern any change in the head wound?" she threw at Mallatt.

"No, my lady. You had it bound well."

"I care not for his look—we may be in for a bout with a fever. It will be best for us to spell one another. I will attend him first. André, how are you feeling? Are you well enough to be up and about?"

The bright curls bobbed eagerly in answer. "Can I remain with you, Mama?"

"No, go with Mallatt—he will see to you—certainly

you must be famished. Let us have no Banbury behaviour and . . . we must play out a little scheme." She came and sat down beside André on the bed. So much had happened to him, how many more games would he play willingly?

Taking his hands, she continued. "The kind people here have made a mistake about all of us and as we were too frozen to speak much, we could not correct them. It will be easier now for us to continue to let them believe what they first thought—do you understand that?"

André did not understand what Mama was talking about but readily agreed.

"Good. Now, they think that all of us are a family—traveling *en famille.*"

André let out a giggle. "They think *Monsieur* Mallatt is *mon père?*"

"No, no," corrected Juliane with a dull blush as Mallatt maintained a stolid silence. "They believe Lord Tretain is your papa—my husband."

She blushed even more at the bout of giggling this induced.

"But, Mama, Papa would never allow me in his private rooms, and never on his bed."

"Yes, I know that," answered Juliane, puzzled why André would be so adamant on that point. Surely he was allowed to see his father other than in the nursery and upon a horse? No time for those considerations now. "You must remember that this is a game—if any of the people here speak of Lord Tretain, you must answer them as if he were your father. Can you pretend this for me?"

André beamed. Another game! Life was much

more interesting with *Tante* than it had been at home, where he was banned from all life but what was found in the nursery and an occasional outing in the saddle. Who would think he would have a new mama and papa in so short a time. Perhaps Mama wouldn't have to worry over a home for them after all. He had overheard the anxious questioning of Cora one night on that subject—not that he had meant to.

"Be a good lad for Mallatt and stay out of Meg's and the others' way. You must be very grown up for me." She tousled his curls and handed him to Mallatt. "His clothing is in the room across the hall."

The orders fell awkwardly on Mallatt's ears. He was, after all, a gentleman's gentleman, and although he had performed numerous nefarious duties in his service with Lord Tretain, acting as nursemaid was not one of them. He looked dubiously from André to Lady Juliane and back to a beaming André, who was all ready for this marvelous adventure. With a slight tremour he went to the door in obedience. Sure as the snow outside was white, he was headed for Bedlam. Glancing back at Lady Juliane, his eyes caught hers. She saw the concern as they moved to the prone figure of Lord Tretain.

"Do not fear," she said. "He seems strong enough and I have nursed many men through worse—relieve me in a few hours."

"Yes, my lady." With a slight bow, he and the lad were gone.

Juliane pulled the lone chair in the room to the bedside. After freshening the cloth on his lordship's brow and stoking the fire, she sat down facing him.

He has a strong jaw, she thought as she watched him. What a large man he would be if he were not so lean. She had noticed earlier that an extra coverlet had been pulled down the lower half of the bed and tucked under his feet, which hung over the foot of the bed. Ah, yes, tall but much too thin. Muscle to him, but not enough weight—certainly not the look of a man who wastes his life traveling, more of the look of the soldier to him. Reflecting on his age, she puzzled more. The grey of his hair belied the youth she saw in his face, especially in that smile of early morn.

Rising to tuck in a hand that had strayed from beneath the covers, she was surprised. It was manicured in proper fashion but tanned and calloused as few hands of the Quality could ever be. Strange, very strange.

Mallatt had said they had just returned from the continent. Could it have been France? She had had the vaguest sense of being followed and observed ever since leaving Rouen; this is what had prompted her to take the children out of the country on her own. Also Cora had had the greatest fear of the baron returning—almost as if he would be very disappointed to find any of his family alive. Juliane considered herself intelligent, not short of common sense, and was at first dismayed at her fears. She had decided before leaving France, however, that she would travel as a family until she reached her uncle's estate and could get some sound advice. But the vaguest of fears had hounded her. When Mallatt had said they had just returned from the continent, her first thought was that he and Lord Adrian had been following them.

This she dismissed out of hand, but she would rely on her intuition and keep her own counsel until she found the lay of Thedford lands.

As the minutes passed, she had less and less time for reflection, as his lordship became increasingly restless and the fever increased steadily.

It took both she and Mallatt to spoon down a small amount of the broth that Meg insisted was the way to health. Deciding they had managed to get as much into him as was possible, she left Lord Tretain in Mallatt's care and went downstairs to see how Leora fared.

Meg was tending to the babe as Lady Juliane entered, carrying the remainder of the broth.

"He would take only a little," answered Juliane to Meg's unspoken question. "I will try again in a short while. How is Leora?"

"Worse, I fear, m'lady. Her breathin' be harder. We can only do our best and leave the rest in God's hands," she offered as consolation.

"Where is André?" asked Juliane, her eyes sweeping the kitchen.

"No need to worry for him. My boys bundled him up good'n proper 'n took him out with them."

Juliane started.

"No need ta worry," admonished Meg severely. "He be not made of fine china and nothin' a boy enjoys more'n a romp in the snow. Ye've plenty on yer mind with the babe and yer lord. Alva, give Lady Juliane some broth and bread—no need ta let yer strength go."

*　　*　　*

Over the next three days Lady Juliane was to hear those words often, and many more motherly admonishments as well. But as the days became one and she alternated between Lord Adrian's bedside and Leora's cradle, she became cloaked with exhaustion. The hours blended together and all her actions, other than the actual handling of the sick ones, became mechanical.

At last Leora was out of danger and a partial weight lifted from her, but still Lord Adrian lay in the grip of the fever.

Her actions toward him had taken a subtle change. In the hours she tended him, she learned much more about him than most people knew, who had been acquainted with him all his life. In his delirium, his babblings ranged from despair at the death of a pup when he was a boy to wild ravings in a French dialect she could not understand. Many of his mutterings were in French and it became apparent to her that he had dwelt on all levels of life in France. If she had been a simpering miss, much of it would have alarmed her greatly, or caused her to blush deeply. As it was, life in India and nursing soldiers had steeled her to most of it. Lord Tretain's ravings were intricately connected with the political foment in France, of this she was certain. He was certainly more than a casual traveler—but what was he?

6

The sun slowly sagged into the mud-dappled, slush-covered horizon. Taking a deep breath, Lady Juliane stepped back inside the cottage, the wafting odors of freshly baked bread and a meaty stew greeting her.

"Is the broth ready?" she asked Meg.

"Aye, m'lady. But ye be eatin' a plate o' m' stew a'fore ye be goin' back up. I'll na take no for an answer—yer gown be hangin' loose enough already."

Juliane blushed as Jove and his sons grunted in agreement. What the family had seen of this lady of Quality put to the wall all they had ever heard, and they had taken her in as one of their own.

"Just a little then. Truly, I am fine and not a bit hungry."

Meg laughed. "A few hours sleep and she's actin' like this be a spell at Bath or some sech place." She shook her head as she pressed Juliane to a seat. "No room for wool pullin' around here. Ye're more'n due for a rest but reckon ye won't be pried from that man o' yern until ye be satisfied he's better. This night should be the test o' that."

"You think so?" asked Juliane anxiously, having had the same thought earlier.

"Aye, it'll be a bad night, I be think'n, but then the worst should be behind him."

"Yes," mused Juliane. Glancing up, she caught sight of Alva playing with Leora before the fireplace. She smiled. "We have so much to be thankful for." The smile wavered and a tear came to the fore. She thought of all that Meg had done, tending Leora through those first two nights. Feeling a comforting hand on her shoulder, she looked around to the motherly face.

"Let's be hearin' none o' that. Eat up—Mallatt will be a waitin'."

Mallatt was straightening the coverlets as Juliane came into the room.

"How is he?" she asked.

"His lordship is more restless. The crisis will be upon us soon."

"He does look more flushed." She handed the bowl of broth to Mallatt and sat on the bedside. Taking Lord Adrian's chin firmly in hand, she began spooning broth between his lips. Succeeding in coaxing him to swallow only a portion of a few spoonsfuls, she laid the spoon in the bowl, sighing.

"I suppose we must be satisfied with that. Have Alva bring up some of Meg's honied water. He seems to take that better, and we must get some liquid into him."

"Yes, my lady." Mallatt paused at the doorway, running his eyes over her worn figure. She cares for him as if he were her own—better than most wives I've seen, in truth, he thought as he watched her replace the snow-filled cloth on Lord Adrian's forehead and tenderly smooth back the tousled hair. His lordship could hardly do better and if he was to get to know her, he could hardly fail to like her, what with the spirit she shows. It would remove him from the marriage mart, which would certainly make life easier and please his mother. Why she'd even have grandchildren to occupy her time.

Yes, smiled Mallatt to himself, if he could contrive it so that they had to spend more time together, they could come to know one another, and then there would be a chance for the match.

Juliane glanced at Mallatt and was struck by the strange look playing on his features.

"Aren't you feeling quite well?" she asked, anxious lest he be taken ill also. He had been her mainstay through the past few days and it was as if he were a retainer of years with her instead of a chance acquaintance. Indeed, it was remarkable how much like a family they were becoming.

"I am fine, my lady. I will return as soon as I've had a bit of rest."

Nodding in reply, she returned to trying to keep the earl covered. "He is much worse; we will both have to stay the night with him—an hour only can you rest."

Mallatt had no sooner left than the earl became very restless. Deducing that she could not control him standing beside the bed, Juliane rushed to the other side and, lifting her skirts, sprang upon it. Taking both his shoulders in hand, she attempted to press him down, urging him to calm himself as she did so.

"Térès, Térès, is it you? Is it you?" With violent force he flung her hands from his shoulders and grabbed hers instead. Fire-lit eyes stared into her own.

"I must . . . you know I must . . ." he espoused wildly.

"Yes, yes, just lie back for a moment. You are not strong enough to go now. Rest. I will call you," she assured him.

He responded momentarily to her voice and, releasing her, lay back. In an instant he grabbed her shoulders again, seemingly in a rage. "You scum, you traitor. I should wrench your neck for you," he spat at her.

"My lord, you mistake me for another," Juliane countered boldly. "You are ill. Lie back now." Lord Tretain was sweating profusely, labouring for breath, but still he kept his brutal grip.

"Release me, my lord. You must lie back," Juliane told him firmly as he continued to stare at her.

Slowly the rage, the wildness, died from his eyes, leaving only the searing heat of the fever and confusion.

Gently she reached up and took his hands from her shoulders. Picking up the snow-filled cloth that had been flung to one side, she smoothed it over his burning face. "Lie back, my lord," she urged gently. "It will be better soon."

He lay back, watching her face intensely as if trying to comprehend who she was.

"You were in a carriage accident, my lord. Close

your eyes, rest," she urged him soothingly. With a grateful sigh, she watched him relax and close his eyes. Taking a deep breath she was surprised to find herself trembling. He was a strong man; the feel of his hands was still on her shoulders.

After waiting a time to see if he would remain calm, she decided it was safe enough for her to go back to the bedside. As she began to move away, his eyes opened and his hand grabbed hers.

"What, my lord?"

"You will stay?"

"Of course, my lord."

He closed his eyes but would not release her hand. She was still sitting thus, atop the bed beside Lord Adrian, hand in hand, when Mallatt returned.

"My lady?" he stated incredulously.

"It is the only manner in which he will be quiet," answered Juliane calmly. "I feel the fever is worsening."

As if in answer, Lord Adrian sat up, flinging his arms wildly. It took all of Mallatt's and Lady Juliane's strength to restrain him. The struggle continued for the better part of an hour—Juliane all the while trying to calm him with her voice. After a last violent effort, he lay back, spent.

All three were wet with perspiration from the effort. Wiping her dripping forehead, Lady Juliane shouted for Meg.

As Meg rushed in, she was met with a barrage of orders.

"Get the fire roaring—we must not chance a further chill now! We must change his lordship's garments and the bedding if we are to come out of this night ahead of the fever. Move quickly now," Lady Juliane snapped.

A quick glance at the earl bespoke the need of hurried action. Meg threw a few logs atop the fire, then hustled from the chamber to fetch clean sheeting for the bed.

As the fire crackled and popped into a roar, Juliane tore the bedding from the empty side of the bed. Satisfied with that work, she came around to Mallatt. "You have a fresh nightshirt ready?"

"Yes, my lady, if you will leave . . ."

"Leave," she snapped. "What do you take me for—I am no simpering young miss. I have cared for grown men before. We must get him out of these wet things, dried, and redressed as quickly as possible. In his state you would be a long time handling even the first by yourself. Meg—you make the bed fresh while we tend to his lordship," she ordered as the woman reentered the room.

Together the two had Lord Adrian disrobed, buffed dry, and regowned as Meg finished making one side of the bed. Mallatt marveled anew at Lady Juliane.

Almost carrying Lord Adrian, they moved him to the dry bedding. While Juliane tucked the covers about him, Meg removed the last of the sweat-soaked bed linens and Mallatt worked furiously to complete the making.

Juliane sat on the bedside rubbing a handful of snow across Lord Adrian's face. Suddenly his hand grabbed her arm, his eyes open wide. A string of vile epitaphs spewed out, shocking even Mallatt. Juliane was taken aback, not so much by the words themselves as by the hatred trembling in the voice. Just as suddenly, he halted and closed his eyes. After tenderly replacing his hands beneath the coverlets, Juliane continued to cool his crimson face with the snow. Meg parted with one last, wondering glance at the pair before removing from the room with the wet linen and bedclothes.

An hour passed with Lady Juliane and Mallatt taking turns with the constant attempts to cool Lord Adrian; Juliane maintained a steady flow of lulling tones throughout.

At last it seemed the crisis had passed. Lord Adrian was much calmer and the flush not quite as pronounced.

Juliane had just replaced Mallatt at the earl's side when he opened his eyes and gazed at her. She smiled reassuringly.

"You are better, my lord. Sleep now; by morning you will feel much improved."

"My angel," he said quietly. "Your voice is from heaven." The grey eyes were only slightly feverish now and held hers steadily. "Who are you? Where did you come from?"

"Hush, now, my lord. Rest. There is plenty of time tomorrow for all the answers you wish." She passed her hand gently over his eyes, closing them.

"Yes, my angel," he answered tiredly, "if you will promise to be here when I awake."

"Of course, my lord. Sleep now."

His hand crept from beneath the coverlet and covered hers. Juliane was startled by the strength of the grasp and by the thrill it sent through her. With her heart beating erratically—caused by the night's work, she assured herself—she returned the grip softly.

Mallatt watched the two silently, a smile creeping over his features. Ah, yes. He would have to connive some way to constrain the two together. If the match can be made, it would curtail my lord's, ah, "ramblings" to a great degree, he thought, and certainly ensure my life a longer span. My age is beginning to tell, the hearth side is much more appealing than the, er, adventures of the past few years. Lady Juliane may be the means to my peace.

"Mallatt, you may go," Juliane said. "Lord Adrian is sleeping peacefully—the worst has passed. I am certain he will sleep well the remainder of this night. I will watch and call you if any change occurs."

"Yes, my lady. Have a care for yourself."

"Oh, of course," she answered absentmindedly as he closed the door.

A while later she eased her hand from Lord Adrian's as if reluctant to do so. "Angel," she thought. None had ever called her such before or even neared such an endearment—or ever will again, she reprimanded herself sternly. Becoming sentimental over the musing of a sick man—call yourself to order, miss.

Walking from the bed to the fireside, she gazed into the fire. A chill stole over her and she shivered. Her gown was still damp. She checked Lord Adrian and then returned to the fire. Stripping down to the buff quickly, she sponged and dried herself. Donning her warm, long-sleeved nightdress, she buttoned it quickly and drew her wrap over it. Dry and warmed, fatigue descended upon her like a thundercloud. Shaking herself awake, she went to the bedside and touched

Lord Adrian's brow. It was definitely cooler, and he looked peaceful.

Barely settled in the straight Windsor, she found herself nodding off. She steeled herself to remain awake, but unavailingly. Catching herself falling from the chair for the unknownth time, Lady Juliane sighed heavily and yawned. Checking Lord Adrian, she found him much the same—breathing easier, sleeping well.

If I could lie down for just an hour, she told herself, I will be able to resume the watch. Yes, that would be better. He will not stir nor realize it.

Having made the decision, she crossed to the other side of the bed and slid in cautiously, lying on the very lip of the mattress. In the middle of admonishing herself for the steadily crumbling state of her moral virtues, she fell soundly asleep.

7

Eyes pressing upon him—the feeling was not a foreign one. Many times in the past Lord Adrian had had such a sensation. It was part of the intricacies of his adopted trade to be able to perceive such occurrences. This time, however, it seemed he was having difficulty adjusting his senses and evaluating his circumstances. He felt he must be abed—evidenced by the softness and warmth; he was almost certain a leg, other than his own, had crossed his, but where he could be was a mystery indeed.

He had been in London, had gone through his meetings with Lord Palmer. Yes, he had completed them; with the reports official, he was to be free for a time. So where? Details ran slowly through his head; the haze was beginning to waft away.

Of course—mental fingers snapped in his head. He had been on his way to Trees. Snow had been falling heavily and then there had been a coach. He could recall falling, the endless sensation of falling. And yes, he remembered, a soft, clear voice that flowed as rich as honey—or had he dreamt that?

The awareness of someone staring remained with him. Tentatively he raised one eyelid, then slowly the other. Dusky as the room was in the early morning light, he could make out little. Giving his head a toss to clear his vision, he took in his surroundings. A crude room he judged it—evidently a farmer's cottage. There was a fire that would need tending soon, some odd pieces of furniture, a small lad sitting on the foot of the bed, and a dark-haired girl beside him. His eyes swung back to the lad sitting cross-legged and wrapped in a shawl. The pale blue eyes were large in the somber visage, the golden curls askance. He did not flinch as Lord Adrian regarded him for a time, then, glancing from the lad to the head beside his, Lord Adrian noticed it was her arm that was the curious weight on his chest.

How did I come to this, he wondered, giving his head a shake. Where is Mallatt?

"Is . . . is *ma mère* ill?" the large-eyed boy whispered hesitantly.

The anxious whisper drew Lord Adrian's attention back to the lad. The French phrase quickened his pulse.

"Why . . ." A finger to the boy's lips caused him to lower his voice. "Why do you ask that?"

"I cannot understand why she should be sharing a bed with you, although there are too few beds here," he added honestly. "*Ma mère* does not sleep with anyone, other than Leora or myself on the ordinary."

68

"She does not?" He tried to keep his tone as serious as the lad's.

A shaking head answered him solemnly.

"Who is Leora?"

"My *enfant* of a sister—she has been making a nuisance of herself by being very ill," he shrugged petulantly.

The boy's accent and use of French phrases continued to arouse Lord Adrian's curiosity. "Where are we?" he asked in a hushed tone. He did not wish to wake *la mère* until he had as much information from the lad as possible.

"I do not know. Some kind people—*fermiers*—are caring for us. Why did your phaeton run into our coach? Do you always drive so carelessly?" the boy asked innocently.

With a wince, Adrian shrugged that aside. "What is your name?"

"André."

"Just André?" He saw the balk come to his eyes. "That is French—*n'est-ce-pas? Où habitez-vous?*"

"*Nous habitons Rouen*—ah, Monsieur—*ma mère* says we must be *anglais* now," he answered, wrinkling his nose as if he did not understand the reasoning behind this.

"Rouen. Is anyone with you besides Leora?"

"There was Cora—*la domestique de ma mère*—always wailing, worse than Leora. After the accident she refused to go on and *ma mère* sent her back with the coachman. That is how we came to be with you," he stated as if this explained all. "Mallatt was most displeased at first. He did not think *ma mère* should do it."

69

Lord Adrian's eyebrow lifted at the familiarity with which André used Mallatt's name.

"You say Mallatt did not want you to come with us?"

"*Oui,* he said you would not care for it and that there was no way for Mama to ride—but Mama said you could not object as you were *insensible.* I have learned that Mama usually gets her way," sighed André wistfully.

"You do say now, interesting. Where is Mallatt now?"

"He sleeps in Jem and Ned's room—although he was with you when I went to bed last night. I sleep in Alva's room."

Deciding there was a lot he had to learn from his surroundings, Lord Adrian elected to try and get to the hub of matters. "What was Mallatt doing in here?"

"Oh, he and Mama have been nursing you for days it seems. You had a fever from lying in the snow too long, Mama says," he answered very knowledgeably. "What a great fuss you raised with your screaming and thrashing about. I heard Meg say Mama would be hammered black and blue from head to toe the way you threw yourself about, not that I tried to overhear her," he added, hanging his head.

"I am certain you did not," Lord Adrian assured André, smiling. "Did you happen to overhear anything else?"

"*Oui,* ah, yes. Meg thinks you are *un mauvais mari.* Dragging us *innocents* about with no maid or nanny to help Mama."

"No doubt," replied Lord Adrian dryly. The announcement that he was traveling *en famille* was only a slight surprise at this point. Hearing footsteps in the hall, he cautioned André, "Tell no one you have spoken to me." He lay back and closed his eyes.

"André, what be ye doing in here?" rebuked a motherly voice. "Your papa has been deathly ill and I wouldna' be surprised if yer mama was on our hands before this be done. Between Leora and yer pap she has slept little these four days past. Sit quietly while I add to the fire—they both need all the sleep they can sum up." The rustle of skirts and thump of logs followed. "Come." Lord Adrian felt André being lifted and then heavy steps went out of the room.

So, Adrian thought, the auburn one beside him was a dedicated nurse—interesting—from Rouen. What had he heard of happenings there? Trying to recall, his thoughts began to swirl together and slowly he dropped back into an uneasy sleep.

Downstairs, Meg was placing breakfast before her family. Lord Tretain's family was much in their conversation.

"Let's be keepin' the gagglin' down," admonished Meg as Ned clanged his spoon into his empty bowl. "Her ladyship needs her rest. Ye should see her—sleepin' like a lamb, the dear soul. From the looks o' her man, he'll soon be in fine fettle again; and 'tis a piece o' reason I'd like to be givin' him then."

"That Lady Juliane is far differn' any o' them ladies o' Quality we've heard tell of," contributed Ned.

They had all come to like and have deep respect for Lady Juliane.

71

"None o' them puttin' on airs, 'cause she be bettern' us neither."

Alva came down the stairs leading André, now fully dressed. "Well, Master André, do ye 'ave appetite or no this morn?" asked Meg sternly.

"I am very hungry, Mrs. Meg," he answered with a bright smile.

"Then to the table with ye. Alva . . ."

She was interrupted by the sounds of horses in the yard. First looking questioningly at Jove, she tried to see who it was.

"They'll be a comin' to the door, woman. I'll see to 'em." He pulled on his heavy cloak and stepped outside. There were six figures. Four were checking over Lord Tretain's phaeton, which the sons had brought to the yard only two days earlier.

Peeking around the door, Meg watched. Two of the man she knew—Jacob and Tom from Time's Crossin', an inn not far from the fork where her men had found Lord Adrian's phaeton. Ah, Jem was bringin' them to the cottage. She could learn who they were and what they were about.

"Warm brew—woman, be quick now. Pardon, yer honour, these are the best we have," Jove said to the man directly behind him.

"Never mind that. What other information can you give about these people?" demanded Squire Preston.

"Nothin', sir. All we know I've told ye—they be Lord Tretain, his wife, and young un's. There was an accident—his carriage tipped over. They got lost tryin' to find the Time's Crossin' and strayed in here—that be five days since and froze near to death they be then."

72

"I must speak with Lord Tretain."

"Beggin' yer pardon, yer honours," interrupted Meg, "but his lordship just passed the peak o' a fever last night. He and his lady be sleepin' and well needin' it. Could ye talk to his man?"

The squire had pulled off his left glove and was slapping it irritably in his right palm. "I suppose so," he agreed distastefully.

"Ned," Meg jerked her head toward their room.

Ned allowed Mallatt no time to fully awaken before dragging him before the squire; he reasoned that since Mallatt was fully clothed, there was no need to wait. He knew his mum would be rare put out if Lady Juliane had to be got up.

Mallatt was valiantly trying to martial his intellect to the fore as he took in Squire Preston's figure. The only thought in his mind was to ask why he was heading for jail.

"You are Lord Tretain's man?"

"Yes . . . my lord. Mallatt."

"You may address me as sir," the squire tossed as an aside. "How is it you came to be here?" he asked, motioning to the surroundings distastefully.

Trying to garner a clue, Mallatt looked around at the others in the room. They seemed as puzzled as he to this questioning.

"There was a mishap, sir, and we found our way here quite by accident."

"Where was Lord Tretain bound?"

"We were going to Trees, my lord's country estate, to visit his mother. She is not well."

"How did your lord's phaeton come to mishap? Is it not rather odd to choose that particular carriage

73

for travel with his family?" Squire Preston inquired diligently.

Mallatt was becoming increasingly uncomfortable. If only he knew the lay of the questioning. "My lord is somewhat . . . impulsive—he wished to travel speedily. It is not for me to question," he finished coldly.

"Yes, yes." The squire waved a hand. He had no wish to offend Lord Tretain, whom he knew by reputation only. The country estate was well known, for it lay less than a day's travel from here. He had not thought Lord Tretain to be married, nor to have children, but then one never knew about these young bucks.

"Did you see anything out of the ordinary as you traveled?"

"Why, no, sir. Why do you ask?"

"A devilish foul deed has been done, my man. As magistrate it is my duty to investigate, but I have sent to London for a runner to help in this.

"A postilion and a lady's maid were found murdered not far from the fork. The postilion had come over three days travel and so was not known in these parts—neither was the woman. The woman's baggage and the interior of the coach were torn apart as if the killers were searching for something of great import to them. Also I have had two reports of strangers being seen in the area, and," he emphasized, "the reports indicate they are French." He let this tidbit of knowledge settle in.

"How much longer do you stay here? . . . Well, man, answer me," snapped the squire, apparently unaware of the effect of his news on Mallatt.

Having lost himself in thought, Mallatt was forced to rouse himself. "Stay here? Most likely not more than another day or two—as soon as my lord is ready and well enough to travel. His mother will be quite concerned."

The squire had, by this time, drained the mug of warm brew Meg had handed him during his exchange with Mallatt.

"Have you seen strangers near here?" he directed at Jove and the boys.

The latter shook their heads negatively in reply.

"No, yer honour" was Jove's contribution.

"Keep your eyes open for any. I have no idea what this business is about. Perhaps this is all there will be to it. We must go on." He turned and stalked out.

For a moment there was stark silence—then everyone began to babble.

"Murder—and not far from here!"

"Did ye pass that coach?"

"What be the world comin' to—a body's not safe anywhere in this wild world of ours."

Mallatt was singularly silent throughout this. Certain that it was Lady Juliane's maid who had been murdered, he wondered what it meant. Perhaps a band of wandering cutthroats out for blunt had done it. The squire could be wrong about their being French. Everyone was ready to see a frog behind anything these days.

How was Lady Juliane concerned in this, if, indeed, she was? It was true she had feared going back from whence she came and the boy's name was French. What had he gotten mixed in?

That Lady Juliane was not a nefarious being, he

was assured. He had worked too closely with her to misjudge that. But, he decided, he had better get the rights of the matter and do so before the squire returned with more questions.

Meg and Jove had noticed his silence, and he became aware of their muted scrutiny.

"I was just thinking how upsetting this will be for Lady Juliane," he offered in explanation. "How does my lord fare this morning?"

"I was up a short time ago and both were sleepin' like babes," smiled Meg. "And there's little reason to go a frightenin' Lady Juliane with tales. Let be for now. Come, join Master André with some porridge."

Mallatt was glad for something to appear busy at; he needed time to think, to sort out his next action.

In the chamber above, Lord Adrian had been roused from his fitful rest by the tramp and stir of the horses in the yard. Recalling where he was, and the information he had garnered from André, he turned to his side, gently removed Juliane's arm, and studied her as she tucked the hand he had removed beneath her pillow.

Gazing down the length of the bed, he guessed her to be tall. He would not top her by more than a few inches. It was difficult to tell, what with the coverlets, but he judged her neither too thin nor too plump. Her face interested him greatly. Tanned beyond what was seemly for a lady, it had an air of honesty about it. Her auburn hair was loose and wispy around her features, softening them, and her mouth was turned in a half smile.

Not beautiful and yet not unpretty, he mused.

Asleep, there was candour in her face. Certainly not the look, or ah, size, of your usual bit o' muslin. It will be most interesting to . . . to become acquainted with the, er, lady, he thought pleasantly.

For many weeks previous, Adrian had not taken time to relax and he was bone weary. Perhaps this was the type of diversion he needed, he thought with a smile. It seemed to suit his acquaintances in London admirably, and certainly the "lady" was willing— why else would she be here beside him now? He could well afford to make it worth her while to return to London with him after he spent a few days at Trees. With two children she should be most grateful for his "protection."

One or two things did nag at him, however. He had noticed she wore the high-necked, long-sleeved flannel gown of virtuous misses—hardly conducive to seduction—and the boy had an air about him that bespoke the Quality, not an urchin of the street. Also the children had said what? Yes—"Meg says you are one *mauvais mari*." Who had given them the idea he was a husband, and why? Mallatt had a great deal of explaining to do.

He continued to contemplate her face; he was after all, snug and she was not unpleasant to view.

As if suddenly aware of someone observing her, Juliane stiffened and opened her eyes. Spice brown stared into cool grey. She relaxed imperceptibly, closing her eyes, and then, just as quickly, sat bolt upright.

"My lord, you are awake," she said blankly.

"That is a reasonable conclusion," he laughed,

catching her hand in his. "Why should that concern you?"

"It does not—no—I am glad to see you in possession of your senses once more." She reached across with her free hand and laid it on his forehead for a moment. "Ah, the fever is gone," she smiled. "We were very concerned."

"While grateful for the care, I am most contrite to have caused such a beauty as you to worry," he winked.

"My lord," she said indignantly as she drew her hand from his angrily.

"Never did I observe a compliment to upset the likes of your sort—come, what must I do for amends?" glibly rolled off his practiced tongue.

"Really, my lord. You presume too much. I know not what gives you the . . ." She halted in mid-sentence, suddenly aware of her position. Blushing profusely, she reached to throw back the coverlets and remove herself.

"Ah, no, my beauty. Surely you mean to do more than warm my bed," he chuckled, gripping her arm.

"You do not understand, my lord. Release me," she gulped.

"I think I understand fully. If you are concerned for blunt, I promise to provide a better love nest in London for us."

Lady Juliane's mouth dropped at these words. Why, he thought her a common—a common—she could not think it. Oh, infamous, and after all her nursing. Anger lit her eyes.

"Oh, you are a beauty," he breathed, as he drew her closer.

"May I remind you, my lord, that you have been ill, very ill," she grated out.

"Then you should be very solicitous of my health and wants. The best thing for my health, now, my beauty, would be a kiss." He was lying back down, drawing her with him.

She scanned the bedside wildly; talk was certainly proving fruitless. The mug which had contained the honied water caught her eye as he released her hands to take her head in his. As he drew her ever closer, she reached wildly for the mug. As their lips met, her fingers touched the mug. For a second she had the wild thought of giving in to his pressing lips. This turbulent thought she flung aside, and clasped the mug firmly, then brought it down on his lordship's head with a dull thud.

It did not knock him senseless, but certainly diverted his attention. As he clasped his head and cursed, she scurried from the bed. Feeling circumstances were completely out of control for the first time in her life, she looked to another for guidance and fairly well screamed: "Mallatt!"

8

Mallatt dropped his spoon in mid-bite at the half-frightened, half-angry scream of his name. There was a brief struggle as he and Meg strove to proceed up the narrow staircase simultaneously. Due to his small size, Mallatt was able to get a leg in first. After the first few seconds of struggle, Meg conceded defeat, and allowed Mallatt to bound up the steps first.

He bolted into the room, expecting to find that Lord Adrian had thrown over his traces. Instead, he was confronted with the sight of his lord sitting up in bed holding his head and Lady Juliane struggling angrily into her wrap. It was not difficult to guess what had occurred.

Lady Juliane greeted Mallatt with a contemptuous glance that blamed him for not warning her of his lord's pandering ways.

Meg was equally taken aback by this look as she stumbled over Mallatt into the room.

"My lady, what is wrong?"

"Mallatt, rid my chamber of these—these people. Get them out—I want some explanations!" commanded Lord Adrian.

"You just be calmin' yerself—what you be meanin' upsettin' your good wife, why . . ."

"Wife!"

"Meg, I think you'd best leave this to me," Mallatt said urgently. "You know the 'Quality.' " He tossed a knowing wink at her.

"Well, I don't . . ."

"Never fear," he soothed. "I am accustomed to these outbreaks. It will be settled peacefully." He turned her toward the door. She shot a glance at Lady Juliane and was somewhat assured by her nod. Glancing suspiciously at Lord Tretain's angry face and back to Juliane, who had turned to face the fire, she sighed. Mallatt propelled her out the door and shut it before she could reply.

Tsking all the way to the kitchen, she gave her family a speaking shrug in answer to their questioning stares.

Upstairs, Mallatt drew a deep breath and mentally girded himself for battle.

"Mallatt, will you please explain to your lord that I . . ."

"Yes, Mallatt," mimicked Lord Adrian angrily, "will you explain how I happen to wake with a cracked skull and a witless wench abed with me who tries to finish the work."

"Perhaps, my lord, it would be far better for you to explain to Mallatt your behaviour," rasped Lady Juliane derisively.

"I do not explain my behaviour to servants," he retorted. "My behaviour! It was not I who came to your bed," his lordship flung back.

Lady Juliane was momentarily silenced by this, and Mallatt deemed it wise to step into the breech.

"Now, my lord, please calm yourself. This can be explained."

"Then do so!"

"The cracked skull came when the phaeton overturned. After the accident, Lady Juliane's postilion refused to go on—in fact he turned about. It seemed most ungracious—even the act of a heartless bounder—to permit the lady and her two small children to be stranded in such weather. What could I do but accede to their coming with us?"

"What could you do indeed!"

"There is no need for you to use such a tone with Mallatt, my lord," interrupted Lady Juliane. "He had little choice in the matter, I assure you."

"And what right have you to say what tone I will use with my servants?" he barked back.

"Every right, my lord, as I am the cause of his being in your 'poor' graces, although I doubt that there is such a thing as being in your 'good' graces," she snapped in return.

"Mallatt, remove this woman before I lose my temper."

"You've already lost much more than that, my lord," pursued Juliane. "Perchance, you wish to remove me yourself, Mallatt certainly is too well mannered. How unfortunate his master is not also."

Mallatt's expression was becoming more pained

upon each word. This was not an auspicious beginning for what he had in mind for the pair.

"Please, my lord . . . my lady—if you could be silent for a moment, I will explain the situation."

Both bit back words and glared at Mallatt for the arrogance of his interruption.

Mallatt proceeded hastily. "At any cause, there was naught but that Lady Juliane and her tykes come with us. Somehow in the dense snowfall, we missed the inn and by some far chance were found by Jove and his sons. By that time we were all near frozen insensible and quite unable to explain ourselves. The good farmer and his wife decided, quite simply, that you and Lady Juliane were man and wife, a natural supposition under the circumstances, and placed you together in this room.

"By the time Lady Juliane and myself had regained our wits, the damage had been done. We could not explain without harming Lady Juliane's reputation. It seemed simpler to maintain the misunderstanding until leaving. At the time there seemed to be little harm that could come to any of us by doing so.

"I might add, my lord, that Lady Juliane nursed you most competently and dedicatedly through your bout with the fever, along with her small daughter. I would imagine," he added with asperity, "that you discovered Lady Juliane abed with you due to the chill of the room and sheer exhaustion. You have been ill several days now," he finished curtly.

Lord Adrian swung his eyes from Mallatt to the glaring Lady Juliane, then back to Mallatt. "And what, in your opinion, should we do now?" he asked sarcastically.

"That, my lord, is your decision, of course. Although," he coughed, "there is an added circumstance you should be apprised of before reaching any decision."

"And what is that?"

Going before Lady Juliane, Mallatt said, "It would be best, my lady, if you would be seated before I continue."

Both Lord Adrian and Lady Juliane wondered what was to be told now. Juliane could think of nothing she needed to be seated to hear. Proceeding to the chair at bedside, she pointedly moved it before sitting down. This action caused the furrows on Lord Adrian's brow to cease somewhat and brought a mischievous glint to his eyes.

"I am afraid this may be sad news, my lady. A magistrate visited the cottage briefly this morning, asking questions. It seems your maid and the postilion were found—murdered."

Disbelief flared on Lady Juliane's features. "There would be no reason for anyone to harm them. Cora was a nuisance but none felt ill toward her—that is, oh . . . well, she had nothing of value."

"Nevertheless, it is true and the squire says there are reports of strangers in the district who are thought to be French."

Both men noticed she blanched slightly at this last word, fear springing into her eyes.

"What can that mean?" she asked shakily.

"I know not, but more to the point, Jove had already told the squire of you, presenting your names as man and wife, and I did not disturb this belief," he ended with half-hearted shame.

"I see," said his lordship. "Either we proceed as you have directed, or we ruin Lady Juliane's reputation, giving rise to a scandal that would send my mother off in an apoplexy; also it would bring the magistrate's full suspicions to bear on the *lady*."

His inflection on the word *lady* brought a sharp glance from Juliane. "You must not extend yourself on my part, Lord Tretain," she said. "It is my own doing that brings me to this predicament and I am fully capable of weathering through it sufficiently on my own."

"Your reputation matters so little then?" asked Lord Adrian chidingly.

"No, my lord," responded Lady Juliane, with a hint of anger replacing her fear. "But I cannot but feel association with you can but do me added harm and I have no wish to place myself in your debt. I am certain Jove would take the children and myself to an inn."

"I am certain of that, also—especially when his good wife learns she has been sheltering what she will believe to be a wanton wench, a bit o' muslin, if you understand my meaning. What type of treatment do you think you and your children will be given when circumstances are known—and known they will be."

Bitterly, Lady Juliane had to acknowledge the truth in what he said. How would she ever find Uncle Thedford? Her coins were few and the gossip would follow her; she knew enough of posting boys and inns to be certain of that. Despair flashed fleetingly over her. Exhaustion still hung heavily about her and this latest incident brought back memories of all they had gone through to come this far.

Lord Adrian felt a twinge of regret at his harshness as he saw the effect it had on her. It was possible he had misjudged her.

Lady Juliane remained silent; reasoning, at the present time, felt like a labour impossible.

"I believe it best," stated Lord Adrian with restrained magnaminity, "that for now we proceed as the pair of you directed. This evening we can discuss what we should do. We may be able to work something out so that we can leave here with Lady Juliane's reputation still 'intact.' Then we will leave her and the children at an inn to continue their journey.

Unfathomably, this struck Lady Juliane as the worst possible decision, even though it was the most sensible and more than she felt she had a right to expect. She could not admit her reluctance to be out of Lord Adrian's life.

Seeing her hesitancy, Mallatt came before her. "It would be best for now, my lady, for you to rest for the remainder of the day. You are much too fatigued to think clearly. We will speak on this after we sup; you will find things will look much better then," he prompted gently.

With practiced restraint Lord Tretain contained his surprise at Mallatt's concern. Never in all their years together had Mallatt exhibited any feeling for the feminine gender, and certainly never for ladies of Quality, not even when his lordship had wished it. That he should be so solicitous of Lady Juliane spoke well for her; he would have to redirect his thinking.

"Yes, you are correct," sighed Lady Juliane, giving Mallatt a look of gratitude that caused a flash of pain to Lord Adrian. "But what of Cora? I must do something, see to proper burial . . ."

"I am sorry, my lady, but if you wish to stay clear of the magistrate, it would be best for you to do nothing. It could prove most embarrassing to you and to my lord. She will be given a proper burial by the district. Had she any family?"

"No, none. My father took her in when she was orphaned on our estate."

"Never mind then, she will be taken care of. His lordship will see to it. Now, go to Alva's room and lie down. You must take care of yourself for the children's sake."

"Yes, Mallatt—you will see to them?"

"Of course, my lady."

Lady Juliane gave him a grateful glance before she left the room, totally ignoring Lord Adrian.

Mallatt closed the door as she left. Bracing himself, he turned to face Lord Adrian, who was eyeing him speculatively.

"I had no idea abigail and nanny were among your many abilities, Mallatt. I have misjudged you."

Untouched, Mallatt replied, "You have misjudged Lady Juliane, if I may say so, my lord, not myself."

"Perhaps. We shall see. What do you know of her?"

"Very little, in fact," answered Mallatt, slightly sheepishly. "But I would stake my life on her being as honest and virtuous a lady as there be. Nothing flighty about her," he defended.

"Enough on that. As I said, we shall see. Where is my lady's lord and who is he?"

Mallatt wove his fingers together behind his back.

"Again my lord, I know nothing. Her abigail addressed her as 'my lady' and she has the look and actions of a lady, born and bred. No mention has been made of her surname—indeed, she seems to go out of her way to avoid it, as if she were fleeing someone or something. Even Master André has nightmares. Then we have the murder of her abigail, and just the mention of 'French' causes instant fear. This could be of interest to you?"

Ignoring the last statement, Lord Adrian replied, "Yes, I noticed the fear. The lad you mention was in here earlier and said they were from Rouen. I know I have heard something about an occurrence there, perhaps something connected even with my work, but I cannot recall it." He frowned in annoyance.

"Most likely due to the fever, my lord. How are you feeling?"

"I would be fine except for this blasted head; at least the mug did not break, splintering me. Fetch me my robe."

"Yes, my lord," said Mallatt dryly.

"Confound it man, how was I to know she was not here willingly?" blurted Lord Adrian.

"Of course not, my lord," agreed Mallatt.

"You know not the woman's origins, her name, or her position, and you would hold her virtue up to me. She is probably some scheming wench out to snare a rich protector."

"Yes, my lord," mumbled Mallatt, suddenly hopeful; he had never seen his lord so put out. "Perhaps you should continue to keep her under observation until we learn the truth."

"What would you have me do," snapped Lord Adrian in vexation, "take her home and present her to Mother!"

Mallatt wisely chose to say nothing.

9

Lady Juliane regained consciousness slowly. Lying absolutely still, she opened her eyes. Pale streaks of light were beginning to pierce the darkness.

How long have I slept? she wondered. It must be morning. In the dim light she spied a cot upon which she surmised Alva had spent the night; nowhere could she see André.

A deep rumbling inside her called attention to the fact that she had not eaten in over twenty-four hours. Well rested, her appetite was once more full blown.

Hearing faint sounds from the kitchen, she decided to rise—Meg would be preparing breakfast. Sitting up, she recalled that all her garments were in Lord Adrian's room. Grimacing at this thought, she decided his lordship would not rise before noon and she could be quiet enough to avoid detection.

Fully awakened by the chilling cold of the floor, she slowly eased open the door to Lord Adrian's chamber. The fire was a heap of dull red coals, but the window allowed enough light for her to make her way safely. Easing the door shut, she edged halfway past the bed, when the sight therein caused her to gasp and stop.

Cuddled next to Lord Adrian, arm flung atop, was André. Astonishment easing, she gazed fondly at the picture the two presented.

"Asleep, my lord, you present a most different impression," she murmured. Shaking her head over it, she made her way to the old wardrobe. Meg had insisted upon placing her garments in it. The door creaked as she carefully opened it and she glanced hastily at Lord Adrian, but he had not stirred. With her back to him she hurriedly removed her nightgown, donned the suitable undergarments and petticoats, and slipped the gown over all—thankful once again that Providence had guided her to purchase a gown with frontal closures. With periodic, furtive glances at Lord Adrian, she was certain he had not been roused.

Fully clothed, hosed, and shod, she flung a shawl about her and made for the door. Pausing once more at the foot of the bed, she stared at the pair therein. She found it difficult to believe that Lord Adrian had actually shared his bed with a small boy. It may be I have misjudged him, she thought. In all candour, his first impression of me could not have been other than what it was.

Perversely, this brought a smile to her lips as she thought of her brother and his new wife. Their reaction to the situation would be completely predictable. They would have them married out of hand. That thought changed her smile to a frown. Had this idea occurred to Lord Adrian? He certainly had not been gentlemanly enough to mention it in their encounter. It would be most unsuitable. Setting her jaw, Lady Juliane went from the room; it would be a most unacceptable solution.

Meg greeted her with a smile as she came into the kitchen. "Bless ye, m'lady, ye should still be abed."

"No, Meg, I feel perfectly restored and," she laughed, "as hungry as the cattle the boys went out to give fodder to."

"Ah, a hearty appetite be the best sign o' health. We needn't be worrin' about ye," she answered, pleased.

"No, indeed. I have always been in good health. How are the children?" Juliane asked, walking toward the cradle.

"Both be hale and hearty. Just be a twit careful o' the babe and ye will have no trouble. Even Lord Tretain be recoverin' as fast as the sun pops o'er the horizon. Mallatt was sore tried to keep him abed the night past. Askin' for ye, real kind like, he was," she added artlessly, as Mallatt had hinted at some trouble between the lord and his lady.

Lady Juliane frowned; she was certain Lord Tretain had been most "solicitous."

Noticing Leora stir, she drew back the blanket that covered her. As she applied herself to removing the soaked nightgear, she asked with seeming innocence, "How did André come to spend the night in Lord Tretain's chamber?"

"Ah," said Meg, stirring the morning's porridge industriously, "I do think that be Mallatt's doings." She chuckled. "He took the lad up with him when he took his lordship's broth to him. When I went up to check on ye an' yer lord, Master André was perched up on the bed listenin' to some tale of yer lord's. Mallatt asked where the boy would be sleepin' seein' as ye were in Alva's bed. I hadna' worried about it and said as much. Master André, he pops up with, 'why don't I sleep with *mon père.'* Mallett, he scolded him serious like, but Lord Tretain stopped him and said the boy could sleep with him. Mallatt acted like this was most displeasin', but ye should o' seen the grin he gave me when he came down later.

"That Mallatt, he's one as has a head on his shoulders." She chuckled once more to herself.

Having gotten Leora to a state of holdable dryness, Lady Juliane settled into the rocker with her. Each began amusing the other.

With hair hanging loose, and engaged in playing with the child, she presented a charming picture to Mallatt as he entered.

If only my lord could see this, he thought. Let us hope that Master André has had the proper effect.

"Good morning, my lady. I am most pleased to see you looking so well. How is Mistress Leora?"

"She is very well, thank you, Mallatt. Were you able to rest enough?"

"Yes, my lady. His lordship continues to improve rapidly, in spite of his head," he added soberly. This drew the smile he wished from Lady Juliane.

"I must go to him now. Master André may have awakened early. Excuse me, my lady."

Juliane's eyes followed him as he left the kitchen.

The oddest notion that he was plotting something nibbled at her—but what could it be?

A shriek of laughter, followed by a profusion of giggles, met Mallatt's entrance into his lord's chamber. He marveled at the sight of Lord Adrian wrestling and tickling André, rolling wildly amid the sheets and coverlets. Beaming at the pair, and congratulating himself on his strategy thus far, he decided there definitely was hope in the situation if he could but smooth the way between the two and contain them together for a sufficient amount of time.

Spying Mallatt, Lord Adrian coltishly heaved a pillow at him, then assisted André in doing the same.

"It is a pleasure to see you so well this morning, my lord," remarked Mallatt drolly, plumping the pillows and returning them to the bed. "Master André, how do you fare?"

"He is very well," answered Lord Adrian ruffling André's curls, "and we are as hungry as two . . . tigers."

"*Oui,* two *tigres—Tante* Ju . . ." he halted fearstricken. "Mama has told me of tigers," he finished clumsily.

"How does your mama know of tigers?" asked Lord Adrian, his interest pricked, especially by the *tante.*

"She saw many of them in India," André replied importantly.

"In India? When was this?"

"*Je ne me rappelle pas,*" answered André with just a hint of stubbornness to let Lord Adrian know he would learn little more.

India, Adrian reflected. That would explain the

unladylike tan. But the children, at least André, were not tanned. Had she been traveling without them? Was her husband in the king's service? He was distracted from further thought as André pounced on him.

After allowing them to wrestle briefly, Mallatt drew André from the bed. With a stout slap to his seat, he instructed him to find Alva and have her dress him.

Giving Mallatt a wrathful glare for interrupting his romp with Lord Adrian, André went petulantly from the room.

"Bring hot water for my shave, Mallatt. I feel fully repaired this morning. Where are my clothes?" Adrian asked cheerfully.

"You will rise today, my lord? That would be most unwise," replied Mallatt, alarmed. How was he to keep the pair together if Lord Adrian insisted upon recovering so quickly?

"Nonsense. Sometimes I think 'most unwise' constitutes your entire vocabulary. Lay out my garments before you get the hot water. What humour do you find my fair 'wife' in this morning?"

Mallatt glanced inquiringly at Lord Adrian. "She seems in fine fettle. I left her amusing the babe, Leora," he responded carelessly.

"Where has she been taking her meals?"

"We have been eating with the family, my lord—that being Lady Juliane's wish and certainly the most practical solution considering the situation," he answered, laying out breeches and waistcoat.

"Not too high in the instep, is she. That is commendable to a degree," stated Lord Adrian as he stood, swayed slightly, and righted himself. He held a hand out, warning Mallatt to stay back. "My water, if you are finished."

"Yes, my lord."

After Mallatt departed, Lord Adrian sat back upon the bed. He was weaker than he wanted to admit and would have to nurse what strength he possessed. Mallatt found him reclining lazily on the bed when he returned.

The bowl of hot water was almost dropped when he was greeted with, "You may shave me now."

"Yes, my lord?"

"Come, Mallatt. You have been aching to tend to me 'properly' for over ten years—now is your moment. You may shave and dress me," Lord Adrian told him matter-of-factly.

This was so out of the ordinary that Mallatt began the task with some trepidation. An hour later found both lord and valet close to wishing the other in Hades.

With the task well-nigh accomplished, Mallatt said with relief, "I am sorry there is no looking glass, my lord. You do look . . . quite well turned out."

Lord Adrian's dress could not be termed dashing, but its cut was superb and the somber hues complemented Lord Adrian's peppered hair and narrow visage. He viewed Mallatt's pronouncement skeptically, but was at a loss as to how to improve his appearance without the aid of a looking glass.

Observing his lord's preening with an optimistic eye, Mallatt judged it a favourable sign. On the ordinary his lord was not so concerned with his looks and there could be but one person in this cottage for which the effort could be justified.

With a grimace of futility, Lord Adrian mumbled to himself.

"Yes, my lord?" asked Mallatt, properly devoid of expression.

Throwing him a distasteful glance, Lord Adrian chose to ignore the question and proceeded down the stairs.

They entered the kitchen simultaneously with Jove and his sons. This coincidence gave rise to much stammering, bowing, and confusion until Lord Adrian raised a hand to silence everyone.

Offering his hand to Jove, he said, "I take it you are Jove. I offer my profound thanks for what you have done for myself . . . and for my family."

Jove stared at the proffered hand, then hurriedly shook it. "Nuthin', my lord. Nuthin'."

An awkward silence followed as the family was not quite certain what to do. It was one thing to sit to table with Lady Juliane, but this buck did not have the look of one who invited familiarity.

Surmising the trouble, Lord Adrian flashed a winning smile at Meg. "Your broth has been most tasteful, but I am famished to the core. Could we not all be seated? I am certain your menfolk have a hearty appetite after an early morning's work."

Lady Juliane rose to join them all at table, uncertainty as to Lord Adrian's action toward her making her steps hesitant. She almost balked when Lord Adrian took the chair Mallatt was holding for her and said, "Good morning, my dear. You are looking quite fetching this morning, as is Leora." He made a brief leg gracefully.

Not trusting herself to reply, she glowered at him and permitted him to seat her.

Mallatt deftly drew out the chair next to her, giving Lord Adrian little choice as to seating.

Lady Juliane watched in amazement as Lord Adrian quickly set the family at ease, speaking with Jove knowledgeably on various agrarian problems, asking the sons questions on hunting, and complimenting Meg's cooking. She could see they were all falling under his spell.

A new side, my lord, she thought. With that beguiling charm you could win over a stone.

But Juliane felt suspicious of his actions and could not reconcile herself to being friendly, despite his repeated efforts toward her.

Mallatt viewed the scene before him with pleasure. To all appearances it was a happy family. Lady Juliane was applying herself to some needlework—a bit too diligently for his purposes he thought; Lord Adrian sat opposite in a comfortable chair claimed from the meager furnishings of the parlour in honour of his presence. He had declined the use of the parlour, deeming it too chilly, much to Meg and Jove's relief as it had become their temporary quarters.

Lord Adrian's attention was divided among contemplation of the fire, Juliane, André, and finally Leora, who was playing on a coverlet near the fire.

André objected occasionally to Leora biting on his tin soldiers—a depleted regiment of six, the only toys he had salvaged from Rouen—but otherwise he was amusing her tolerably.

Leora tired of this soon and struggled up. She

glanced about the room and then made straight for Lord Adrian. Grasping his knees, she cooed up at him. He turned his reflective gaze from the fire, and smiled briefly at the happy babe.

Lady Juliane laid her work aside and called, "No, Leora, come here. Come."

"No." Lord Adrian surprised himself as he reached down and drew Leora to his lap. "She is fine."

"But, my lord," began Juliane, then desisted as he shook his head.

To Lord Adrian's consternation, Leora found it great fun to destroy his cravat and chew on one end of it. He suffered this and many tugs on his shirt-front lace, much to Mallatt's surprise. He could never remember his lordship taking much interest in children, much less allowing them on his person.

Marking Lord Adrian's attention to Leora, André dropped his toy soldiers and ran to climb aboard also. Another shake of his head stifled Lady Juliane's protest and soon he had both children laughing wildly as he tickled and coaxed them with all manner of silly faces.

Watching them, everyone else in the room was soon chuckling, including Juliane. No one who could amuse the children so expertly, could be all bad, she decided. Looking at her across the heads of the children, Lord Adrian nodded approvingly. "So happy to see you in better spirits, 'my dear.'"

She started to frown at him, then clapped a hand over her mouth to still a laughing gasp.

Lord Adrian was confounded by this for a moment. Then, looking down to find the source of an unexpected warmth on his leg, he froze at the sight of a slowly spreading stain.

His expression caused Juliane to burst into unrestrained laughter as she rose and took Leora from his lap.

Puzzled as to the cause of Lady Juliane's sudden gaiety, Meg rose from her mending and drew near. She quickly spied the stain on Lord Adrian's leg, and tsking loudly took Leora from Lady Juliane and called Alva to take Master André. "Bedtime for all, I do think," she said.

Juliane sat down, weak from laughter. It had been a true release to enjoy a good laugh. She could not recall the last time she had laughed so hard. Becoming aware that Lord Adrian was closely observing her, she tried to achieve a look of proper chagrin. "I tried to warn you, my lord."

"I would not deny myself such a novel experience," he said dryly, "when it produces such a lovely hue to your cheeks."

Blushing, she became wary. Compliments of this sort were not commonly hers. Suspicion passed visibly over her features, causing Lord Adrian to wonder at its origin.

"Do you desire me to assist you, my lord?" asked Mallatt.

Lady Juliane's reaction to this question brought an impish gleam to Lord Adrian's eye.

"We will manage, won't we 'my dear'?" he replied, rising and taking her by the arm.

She opened her mouth to object, but it dawned unpleasantly that she could not do so without revealing the deception. Trying to ascertain just what course lay before her, she absently allowed Adrian to lead her to the stairs. At the foot of the stairs she looked furtively at Lord Adrian and then to Meg. "I must see to Leora and André."

"Meg, you would not mind tucking them in this eve, would you?"

"Of course not, my lord. You go right up," she replied, smiling broadly.

Lord Adrian swallowed the chuckle caused by the panic in Juliane's face. He guided her to the bedchamber, leaving her standing just inside the door, as he shut it and walked to the scarred wardrobe. Removing his jacket, and unbuttoning his waistcoat, he turned to her. She spoke first.

"How do you propose to spend the night, my lord?" she asked coldly.

"Comfortably."

"Comfortably? My lord, you must realize that to stay this night in this room could not but destroy my reputation."

"Indeed? In the eyes of all, your reputation was in shreds the moment we were placed abed together. I do hope your lord will not be too pettish about that," he added, turning back to the wardrobe to place his waistcoat inside. He drew the remains of his cravat from his neck and let it drop.

As he began to unbutton his shirt, Juliane asked in disbelief, "Truly, my lord, you do not mean to disrobe?"

"I do not make it a habit to place my nightshirt over my garments," he assured her cooly.

"You are unspeakable. Is there not the least gleam of gentlemanly manners about you?" Striding to the door, she grasped the knob only to find her hand enclosed in an iron grip. She felt his breath and her heart lurched.

"You know I cannot remain in this room," she said with false calmness.

"Do I?" Removing her hand from the knob, he turned her toward him; their eyes held—hers a mixture of fear, anger, and uncertainty; his, only guarded coldness. "I mean you no harm. Tomorrow we will leave here. The Red Fox is in Wendon, only slightly out of our way to Trees. We will leave you and the children there safely and no one ever need know of the past week or of this night."

"I cannot remain the night in this room," she repeated.

"And where shall you go? If it be downstairs, Meg will only send you back. She values marriage, you know."

"Then neither of us shall have any sleep."

"Oh, no, my beauty. If you wish, you may remain awake, but you will not dictate how I shall spend the night."

"Of course not, my lord. Your wife is most fortunate you choose to be from her; I cannot see how she abides your presence."

"I have none."

"Then you are making some fortunate woman very happy—by sparing her the odious pleasure," she replied sharply.

"Would that I could return the compliment, my lady, but as you travel alone, your husband's wisdom is evident."

Anger sparked from both pairs of eyes as they confronted one another. Lord Adrian was struck with the sudden realization that he wished for nothing but to enfold her in his arms and silence her with kisses. He turned sharply, dropping the hand he had continued to hold, and stalked to the wardrobe.

Lady Juliane let out a slow breath of relief as he did so and silently left the room.

"M'lady, what be wrong? Can I help you?" asked Alva, startled by Lady Juliane's entry into her room.

"Yes, Alva. I left my nightdress here this morning. Also I think it best that I spend the night here. Lord Adrian is a very light sleeper and I wish for nothing to disturb him. We must ensure his complete recovery."

"Oh, yes, m'lady." She looked about, uncertain as what to offer Lady Juliane.

"If you do not mind, I will sleep with André. We have done so before, have we not, André? Perhaps it will keep the nightmares away?"

"Yes, Mama—but could I not sleep with Papa instead, as I did last night?"

"No." She softened her tone. "He must not be disturbed—you toss much too wildly."

André nodded reluctant agreement, then wiggled further beneath the coverlets.

In a short space the cottage was still, everyone abed. Sleep came quickly to most, the only exceptions being a man who was contemplating how a pair of vixen eyes and dark hair that glittered in the firelight could draw him so; and a woman who was wondering how it was that cool grey eyes and decidedly erratic and ungentlemanly behaviour did not repel but attract.

As the moon rose higher, sleep claimed even this unsettled pair.

10

The snow was thickly crusted through the past few days' melting and nights' freezing. Try though they might, the three stealthy figures could not suppress the crunch of their footsteps as they approached the farm cottage. Making their way to the door outside the kitchen, they huddled briefly to resolve a disagreement.

The difficulty settled, they entered easily—Jove having never installed a lock upon the door. Feeling their way carefully, they searched the room—becoming as statues at an unexpected metallic crumple.

"Ce n'est qu'un jouet soldat," whispered the culprit, kicking the flattened toy into the fire.

Two men remained in the kitchen while the third inched his way up the stairs, managing to suppress all but an occasional squeak.

Pushing open the door of the first room he came

to, he entered warily. The moonlight afforded enough light for him to view the contents of the room.

A malevolent smile lit his face as he caught sight of André's curls next to Lady Juliane's. Stealing around the bed, he jerked the covers aside and scooped the sleeping boy into his arms.

Sleep-dazed, André offered no resistance, but the movement of the bed roused Lady Juliane. Seeing the silhouette of the man as he strode around the bed carrying André, she threw the coverlets from her and leaped in front of him. He butted her aside with his shoulder, making for the door.

"Stop," she shrieked, as she picked herself up and pursued him.

"Mallatt! Mallatt! Stop him," she screamed as she lunged at the man in mid-stair.

The thudding of their tumble down the remainder of the stairs, together with André's cries, aroused the household.

A stream of curses emitted from the man, who was trying to restore his grip on André. The boy had assumed a death grip on Juliane in the entangled mass at the foot of the stairs.

Nightshirt flapping, Lord Adrian ran down the stairs. Mallatt and Jove stumbled into the kitchen.

Routed, the intruders made for the door. The first out let loose a loud whistle and muffled hooves came quickly into the yard.

Ned and Jem pell-melled into the kitchen, and all the men gave chase, but they were not fast enough.

Meg was lighting a candle as the men re-entered, eager to shield their bare feet and scantily clad bodies from the cold night air. Lord Adrian led the pack, going immediately to Lady Juliane and André. The boy was still hysterical despite Juliane's efforts to calm him.

Kneeling, he tried to take André from Lady Juliane. André howled, but casting a fear-ladened look, saw that it was Lord Adrian. Relief and trust erased the fear from his features and he loosened his hold on Juliane and dove into Lord Adrian's arms.

By this time, Meg had soothed Leora, somewhat diminishing the pandemonium. The others clumped around the three at the foot of the stairs.

Rising, Lord Adrian held André tightly with one arm and reached out with the other to help Lady Juliane. "Are you all right? Did he harm you?" he asked anxiously.

"No," she answered shakily. "We were not harmed."

"What happened?" was echoed by all.

"I don't really know," parried Lady Juliane. "I awoke to find a man carrying André from the room—I have no idea why."

"Who could they have been?"

"His cursing, it be foreign—be it French?" asked Jove.

It was as if a knell sounded in the room; all thought of the murdered abigail and postilion. Juliane moved unconsciously closer to André, her fear evident.

Seeing it, Lord Adrian encircled her shoulders with his free arm. "Mallatt, get dressed and stand guard. Jove, could your sons relieve him during the remainder of the night?"

"Aye, m'lord. I canna' understand what they'd be a wantin' here—or with yer lad."

"Probably ransom," Lord Adrian tossed out, suddenly feeling very protective of the two within his hold. André's look of trust had gone straight to his heart and he realized that Juliane's call to Mallatt for aid had pained him.

He felt Juliane shiver and, becoming heedful of everyone's lack of attire, he said, "We cannot stand about like this. We will discuss this in the morning. Come, Juliane. Meg, please care for Leora." He slipped his hand beneath her elbow and guided Lady Juliane up the stairs. At mid-stair he called over his shoulder, "I doubt they will return this night, but keep a close watch."

At Alva's door, they halted.

"It would be safest for André to come to bed with me, if you are not afraid," he said quietly.

Lady Juliane tried to search his face in the darkness. "No, I am not," she answered slowly. "Perhaps, that would be best. Do you wish to go with Lord Adrian, André?"

"*Oui*," came the quivering reply.

"As you wish then," she said, turning to enter Alva's room. Lord Adrian's hand stayed her.

"In the morning we must talk—have no fear for this night. You and the children will be well protected."

The earnestness of his voice appealed for her trust and it would have been freely given had she not recalled that the rantings of his delirium linked him to things French.

The entire household slept lightly, and sunrise found all but the children awake. Only Lady Juliane kept to her bed. What could she tell Lord Adrian?

She wished to unburden the entire matter to someone, but could he really be trusted?

If only I could place my faith in him completely, she thought. Why do I have this unreasonable fear? What could they want with André, and who, in truth, are they? The baron? Surely, he would not steal his own son. Her ruminations were interrupted by Alva.

"M'lady, beggin' yer pardon, but his lordship says ye must be risin'. He plans on leavin' before midday," said Alva, almost tearfully.

"Leave before midday? Are you certain he said that?" asked Lady Juliane, sitting up abruptly.

"Yes, m'lady. He was a tellin' Mallatt to get the family's things packed and was askin' me da about the horses."

Lady Juliane's heart sank. So, he was eager to get her problems out of his domain. What else could she have expected? He had no reason to be concerned for her or the children. This thought upset her far more than her fear had done.

Rising and dressing resolutely, she decided it mattered not. She could proceed ably, as she had been doing, with no need of his or any other man's aid.

Later that morning Mallatt was upstairs packing, Lord Adrian was outdoors supervising the handling of his prancers, and Lady Juliane was tending Leora with a heavy heart.

"We be sorry to see ye go, m'lady," said Meg sincerely, as she finished the breakfast dishes. "If ever we can be o' help—ye know ye be welcome here."

"Thank you, Meg. You have done so much for me," she choked and bowed her head as tears dropped on Leora's gown.

Meg came to her and engulfed her in a warm embrace. "Now, now. Everythin' will be fine. Ye'll see. That lord o' yern truly cares for ye and the wee ones." She patted Lady Juliane's back. "Ye'll be feelin' better when ye get to yer home. Tired and overanxious ye be now."

Lady Juliane finally managed to free her kerchief from her pocket and wiped her eyes. "Yes, of course," she sniffed, angry at her weakness. "I am only tired." There was no need to worry Meg, who could not help her. Someone at the inn would surely have heard of Uncle Thedford.

At the sounds of steps at the door, the women drew apart. Lord Adrian entered briskly.

"I will speak with you, now," he said to Juliane, gesturing toward the stairs.

Knowing not what she would say, only that this was inescapable, Juliane went without argument.

Mallatt looked up from his work as they entered. He noted that Lady Juliane was pale but calm and that his lordship had a determined air about him.

"You should not be bothering with our things, Mallatt. I will tend to them," stalled Lady Juliane.

"I do not intend to be delayed—continue, Mallatt. Now," he said, motioning for Juliane to take the lone chair in the room, "we will talk. Why was an attempt made to kidnap André?"

She looked steadily into his assessing eyes. "I do not know, my lord. There is no reason that I know of."

"Are you running from your husband?" he asked coldly.

"I . . . I have none."

110

This response drew a lifted eyebrow from Lord Adrian.

"Please," she said, rising, "desist from these questions. You will be quite free of me when we reach the inn. How soon will we depart?"

He watched her closely. "I have not yet decided whether I should leave you at the inn. I am certain you are in some sort of trouble; will you not let me help?"

His quiet, gentle tone calmed her. If he meant well, he could assist her in finding Uncle Thedford. Before she could come to a decision, a sudden clamour caused by the entrance of a crested traveling coach, drawn by three teams drew Mallatt to the window. Lord Adrian joined him.

"Damnation! It's Mother!"

"Your mother? I am ruined for certain," Lady Juliane said, falling back into the chair with a look of hopelessness.

Without acknowledging why, Lord Adrian determined this would not be so. "We shall continue the deception. You and the children will be safe at Trees until I can unravel this."

"Are you mad, my lord?" Juliane asked blankly.

"Blessedly so," he laughed. "This will be fit punishment for Mother for hounding me all these years to marry. Mallatt, we had better get our story—let me see—we were married in France—perfidity kept me from revealing it. Yes," he smiled, warming to his theme, "Mother will love instant grandchildren. After I have unraveled your mystery, we will leave Trees. Mother will leave me in peace for some time—she may never need to know we never were married."

"He is mad," Juliane said to Mallatt.

"Undecidedly so at times, my lady," he agreed. "Best to humour him. One never knows what turn he will take when one of these spells hits him."

"Mallatt, finish the packing speedily," Adrian ordered. "Juliane, if I see him first, I will send André up. Instruct him to continue in calling me Papa. I must go greet Mother before she demolishes our fine friends."

"Wait, my lord," Juliane said chillingly as he reached the door. "I cannot consent to this. If you will not, I must explain to your mother."

"Mallatt, put some reason into her head before I return with Mother," he snapped curtly, and departed.

Lady Juliane turned incredulously to Mallatt. "He does not mean it?"

"On the contrary, my lady, when he gets that particular look, there is no stopping him."

"But, to use us to play such a cruel hoax on his mother . . ."

"No, my lady, it is your welfare he is concerned with. This will not do his mother any harm." He rolled his eyes expressionably. "He will explain all upon resolution of your troubles, never fear. Come, would it not be best for you and the children to do as he says?"

Lady Juliane paced. They could hear upraised voices below—obviously Lady Tretain had met her match in Meg. Lord Tretain's voice could be heard stilling the others—then steps sounded on the stairs.

Wringing her hands, Lady Juliane turned to Mallatt. "Oh, I cannot. It would be too infamous." She turned to the door, straightening her shoulders.

Mallatt shrugged ruefully. He truly did not like doing this, but she was leaving him little choice.

Opening the door, Lord Adrian's look turned to concern, for Mallatt was gently placing an unconscious Lady Juliane on the bed.

11

"What has happened?" demanded Lord Adrian, rushing to the bedside.

"Just a fainting spell, my lord," answered Mallatt calmly. "You know how overtaxed her ladyship has been these days past."

"This is what you mean to present to me as a daughter?" purred Lady Tretain snidely.

Ignoring her, Lord Adrian continued his anxious check of Juliane. She was not overly warm, her pulse appeared normal. That she had been getting too little sleep during his illness, he was certain; but she was robust—certainly not in the swooning style. Glancing to Mallatt, he noticed his unconcern.

Bending near, Mallatt whispered, "You requested I implant some common sense, my lord. This," he nodded at a small piece of padded firewood lying on the floor at bedside, "was the only variety that presented itself as having a chance for some degree of success." Kicking the firewood beneath the bed, he added, loud enough for Lady Tretain to hear, "Lady Juliane carries neither hartshorn nor vinaigrette with her."

"Satter," Lady Tretain ordered the abigail that was hovering nervously behind her, "fetch my vinaigrette from the coach."

"Would you happen to have carried any laudanum with you, Mother?" asked Lord Adrian, conscious of his mother's constant ailments. She might never use it, but believed one must have the necessary props if one was to be successful. "I believe Juliane would be better for some."

Not the thing to do to her, he thought, but then it would be to her benefit. Once they arrived at Trees she would be impelled to confide in him.

"Ma mère! Ma mère!" André screamed, throwing himself on the bed. He began shaking Lady Juliane with all his might. *"Ma mère!"* Tears coursed down his cheeks.

Lady Tretain stared in wonder at his panic—what was this?

"André. André, listen to me." Lord Adrian had him by the shoulders. "Mama has only fainted. Do you hear me, there is nothing wrong."

André searched Lord Adrian's face. Evidently satisfied in what he saw, he reached out and clung to him.

Holding the boy close and patting him gently on the back, Lord Adrian could only wonder what terrible event had put such fear in the child. He gazed at Lady Juliane. If only she would trust him.

The scene before her was almost more than Lady Tretain could credit. The wild tale of her son being

115

injured and staying at a farm cottage with a wife and family, she had easily scoffed at. Was it intuition then that made her insist on proceeding at once? She still felt that it was impossible for her son to have been married and with children all these years. Why would he have kept the heir from his home? But, she thought, the boy does go to him as to a father, and if it is not love that lights his eyes when he looks on that "woman," I am TOO old. Best to tread warily until I know the lay of things.

"Mallatt, are you finished packing?"

"Yes, my lord. The task is completed."

"Mother, will you allow us to travel with you?"

"Naturally, my son. When word reached me of your illness, I came expressly to care for you—and I but recently from my own sickbed," she said pointedly. Seeing that that was having little effect, she continued, "You will understand I could not be persuaded of the truth of this supposed family you have with you.

"Give it to me, Satter," she commanded as the abigail re-entered the chamber. "I will attend to—is it Lady Juliane?—myself."

Lord Adrian smiled. "Doing it a bit too brown, are you not, Mother?"

Ignoring his words, she held the vinaigrette beneath Lady Juliane's nose. Her son was annoyingly more like his father every day.

Lord Adrian sat André upon the bed and edged his mother aside as Lady Juliane opened her eyes. "Have the laudanum ready, Mother. I do not wish to have her become overexcited."

With the world swirling before her eyes, Lady Juliane shut them tightly, then slowly opened them once more. The swirl slowed till Lord Adrian filled her vision. He looked so concerned that she smiled warmly. The smile faded as the throbbing of her head impinged upon her senses. Raising a hand to her head, she asked uncertainly, "What happened?" Feeling the lump that had already risen on the back of her head, the answer came and anger flared.

Seeing the sparks fly, Lord Adrian deemed it wise to still them as quickly as possible. "Here, swallow this," he said as he forced a generous spoonful of laudanum into her mouth.

Grimacing at the taste, she coughed. "What was that?"

"It will soothe your nerves, my dear," a frigid voice told her.

The most formidable woman she had ever seen entered Juliane's vision as she turned her head toward that voice. Her only thought was that the massive and elaborately powdered periwig could not possibly be made of the woman's own hair. It must be imagination, she assured herself—no one traveled dressed so.

"Mama," said André softly, creeping close to her.

"I am fine, André, never fear," she comforted him.

In attempting to sit up, she found things swirled once again and did not resist as Lord Adrian pressed her back to the bed.

"What did you give me?" she asked accusingly. Passing her hand before her eyes, she became alarmed. Sleep was beginning to overwhelm her; it was hard to think. "How am I to care for the children?" she asked, panic putting an edge to her voice.

"They will be well taken care of. Meg has agreed

117

to let Alva come with us during our visit to Trees. Matters are taken care of—rest now. We will be home soon."

"With us? Home soon?" It was so difficult to reason. "Home? Judith—the children, I must . . ." she drifted into sleep.

"What is she rambling about?" asked Lady Tretain, who could not make sense from Lady Juliane's mutterings.

"It is nothing," dismissed Lord Adrian. "Mallatt, her cloak—and then fetch a rug from the coach. I do not wish to risk her taking a chill.

"Meg!"

The short time that elapsed between his call and Meg's entrance, proved she had been hovering close by, disliking to desert Lady Juliane with such a harridan descending upon her. Coming into the room, she saw Juliane and gasped.

"It is all right, Meg. We gave her a draught to help her rest. You know how much she has been overexerting herself of late. Will you have Alva ready the children? Are the warming bricks ready yet?"

Meg eyed those in the room with mistrust. Lady Juliane had not been happy with the idea of going on. Were these people to be trusted? "The bricks be ready," she said slowly. "Be ye certain her ladyship be all right?"

Lord Adrian went to Meg. Putting a hand on her shoulder, he looked directly at her and said, "I promise you, she will have only the best of care from now on."

"Ye make sure o' that, m'lord," she choked, turning to call André to come with her.

With Mallatt's aid, Lord Adrian wrapped Lady Juliane in her cloak. His mother had seated herself on the lone chair during this procedure. After Mallatt went for the rug, mother and son assessed each other.

"Is she your wife?" asked his mother, coming directly to the point.

"Would I travel to Trees with her if she were not?" he parried.

"I know not," she sighed. "I am an old woman and not well. You have tried me sorely these years past. I trust you have enough feeling for your heritage, if not for me, not to play such a farce."

"The rug, my lord," intoned Mallatt, returning.

"Let us wrap it about her. I will carry her—you take the remainder of the baggage. Don't give me such a look, I am completely restored and trust I can manage," he snapped at Mallatt's hesitancy. He lifted Lady Juliane into his arms. "Mother, if you will."

Lady Tretain rose and swept haughtily from the room. If her son would not confide in her, she would soon see how this "wife" withstood her "welcome."

Alva and the children were settled in the light carriage in which Lady Tretain's servants traveled by the time Lord Adrian's party reached the yard. His mother, being handed into her coach, ordered Satter to accompany the children.

Lord Adrian handed Lady Juliane to two of the coachmen—she was not a bit of fluff. Entering the coach, he directed them to hand her in. Their faces were passive, but their minds were busy storing all these delicious bits of information; they had a wealth of news for the staff at Trees.

"Mallatt, you drive the light carriage. Mind you, keep the pace easy.

"Meg, Jove—thank you for your kindness. I will take care that Alva is happy. You will be rewarded," he called from the interior of the coach.

"God speed to ye, m'lord," Jove answered.

The footman closed the door at Lord Adrian's nod and they started up.

The interior of the coach was richly appointed and thickly padded with velvet cushions for warmth. Lord Adrian settled Lady Juliane back amongst these. Making himself comfortable in the opposite corner, he eased her down so that her head was in his lap. After tucking the rug carefully around her and arranging the warming bricks to his satisfaction, he lifted his feet and placed them leisurely on the seat he faced.

Lady Tretain hurumphed at this as she moved her skirts to avoid having them soiled.

"Three teams, Mother?" was all he said before leaning his head back and closing his eyes.

There was much to sort out. Was he being the fool? Opening his eyes, he looked down at the tumble of auburn hair. She raised a warmth within him that he had not felt for a woman since . . . well, for a long time. There was such an appealing innocence, an earnestness about her—he brushed back a straying tendril and laid his arm across her shoulders. He had been deceived once in the past and yearned to know if he would be again.

Closing his eyes once more, he relaxed. She had not

120

once mentioned marriage and she could easily demand it under the circumstances. This was surely a sign in her favour. Yes, this time it would be different, if she would but trust him.

Lady Tretain had watched her son for some time. It was still difficult to believe he had a wife and family, despite the outward appearance of such.

Why was this "Lady Juliane" unconscious and why did he wish to keep her so?

The girl did not seem to be in his general line—or what he had led her to believe was his line. Her gown was simple. She did not seem to possess a periwig and she had no abigail. The latter fact was the most damnable—no lady of Quality would dare travel without an abigail and, most certainly, not without a nurse for the children. Why, in her day—but this was not her "day" and it was her duty to make sure her son was not making an utter fool of himself over some chit. She would have to see how far he would go.

Dusk was closing in when the coach halted. Lord Tretain was alert instantly. He relaxed as the coach door opened and the coachman said, "With your permission, my lord, we will rest the horses before proceeding further."

"Very well. I believe Meg packed food enough for all of us. It would be in the light carriage. Have Mallatt bring the basket to us."

"Yes, my lord."

Lowering his feet to the floor, Adrian said, "I hope you do not mind a cold collation, Mother."

"Do I have a choice?"

"One would think you were not pleased with me," he smiled.

"Long ago you grew accustomed to my not being pleased with you. I have never known it to alter your behaviour."

"But Mother, I have only done what you have urged upon me for these past years," he answered innocently.

Lady Juliane stirred as Mallatt appeared, ending this brief interchange.

"André has been asking after her ladyship, my lord. Would it be permissible for him to join you for your repast?"

"Yes, bring him. Mother, where did you place the laudanum?" he asked as Juliane stirred again.

"It is not healthy to keep her drugged. You cannot do so indefinitely. Why do you fear having her conscious? Is she that much of an embarrassment?"

"NO!"

His tone and accompanying look startled Lady Tretain; she was inured to his disobedience, but he had never before been disrespectful.

"I know what is best for . . . my 'wife.' I wish her to sleep until morning. She was unduly concerned over meeting you and I will not have her upset."

"Not have her upset? Of all the upstart . . . You descend upon me with a 'family' and care not how it affects me—I am to welcome them with open arms. What of her family? Is her background correct?" she staccatoed.

Lord Adrian tightened his hold around Juliane as if to ward off blows. "I did not descend upon you, rather it was the other way," he said icily. "We have not gotten along well in the past, Mother, to my regret. But do not cross me in this. I will not have her harmed by anyone. Do you understand?"

"My lord," came a call from without.

"Yes? Ah, André—here take hold. That's right. Now sit beside your *grandmère*."

He smiled at the boy's startled look. "She will not eat you. Are you hungry? Mother, will you find something for him?"

Lady Tretain opened the basket. Finding bread and cheese, she passed a piece of each to André, who took them gingerly.

"Why do you stare at me so?" she snapped, still angry with Lord Adrian.

"I have never had a *grandmère* before and you . . . you are so . . . *magnifique*. Can it be you are truly Papa's mama?" he asked incredulously.

Softening at his openness, she laughed. "Yes, André, I am Lord Adrian's mama. And you, where did you learn the French expressions?"

"But where else, *Grandmère*—at home," he answered, puzzled.

She looked to Lord Adrian for explanation.

"André and Leora were born and raised in France."

"Your 'wife' is French? She cannot be."

"No, she is as English as you and I. Circumstances . . . deemed it wise for her and the children to remain in France until now. Let us eat—it will be very late when we arrive at Trees."

It was near midnight when they did arrive. In the moonlight Trees was magnificent.

Built in Elizabethan times, it had been expanded wisely and lovingly over the years. His own father had made several improvements in the interior, mainly to ensure the comfort of the dwellers. Lord Adrian wished Juliane could be awake to get this first breathtaking glimpse as they rounded the tree-lined drive and the house emerged into full view.

He yawned as the coach halted before the main steps.

The children and Alva had to be awakened by Mallatt, as did most of the household; none had imagined her ladyship would return at such an untoward hour. They were startled further to learn that the master was with her, and more, that he had a wife and two children with him—what wonder was this?

"I gather you have kept the master bedroom in readiness for your 'victory', Mother."

"You will not . . ."

"See to it that the countess's room is in all readiness," he cut her off coldly. "We shall be here for only a brief visit but I want my wife afforded all the respect due her. We shall place the children in the two rooms across from ours—they will be quite suitable for a temporary nursery. Juliane would wish the children near her as they are quite easily frightened. Will you see to the orders for me?" he asked conciliatorily.

"As you wish," Lady Tretain answered coldly. "It will take a few moments. I will instruct the fire to be added to in the small salon. You may be comfortable there until the rooms are ready."

"And, Mother," he said, a thought reaching him.

"Yes?"

"Do you have a young servant girl who would be capable of acting as Juliane's abigail? She need only be trustworthy."

"I will ask Mrs. Soams to recommend someone. Everyone here is trustworthy," she added, insulted to the core.

Lord Adrian left Lady Juliane in the hands of Satter and a young girl called Bess. Feeling they would settle her safely into bed, he went to check on the children.

Alva, although slightly overwhelmed by the size of Trees and the stateliness of its furnishings, was nevertheless carrying on efficiently with the children.

"If there is anything you need for the children or yourself, all you need do is ask for it."

"I be havin' all I be needin', my'lord. 'Cept, could it be that a cradle could be found for Mistress Leora? She could fall from these huge beds."

Lord Adrian stepped into the hall and instructed the liveried man he encountered there to fetch a cradle from the nursery. "It will be here soon," he said, returning to the room.

"André." He went to the bedside and tousled the yawning boy's curls. "Sleep well—we will speak in the morning. You are good at games—*non?* We mustn't let *Grandmère* know our secret yet."

André nodded and curled into a ball.

"Good night." Lord Adrian leaned down and kissed the smooth forehead.

He was rewarded with a hug and a kiss. "Sleep well." Going back to Alva, he asked, "How is Leora? Is there any sign of her cough returning?"

"No, m'lord. Me mum sent some of her makin's along if it should be back, but she be fine."

He gazed down at the babe. Noticing for the first time how she resembled Juliane, he felt the desire for paternity. If only they were mine, he thought, leaving the room.

Mallatt had finished laying out Lord Adrian's things in the master suite and Lord Adrian quickly undressed and washed himself. Finished, he drew his richly quilted, brocade robe over his nightshirt. "What is worrying you, Mallatt? I will do the girl no harm."

"It is not that, my lord. I believe we were followed, although I cannot be certain."

"Followed! So they have not given up." He paced. "If only we knew what or who was pursuing them. Have Holdt get two able-bodied men to stand guard outside the children's room—we cannot be too careful." He waved dismissal.

Preoccupied, he stood where he was for a long time after Mallatt had left. Then, purposefully, he opened the door to the short passageway connecting the master bedrooms.

"My lord," bobbed Bess. "Her ladyship is abed and sleeping well. Do you wish me to stay the night with her?"

"No, that will not be necessary. Allow her to sleep as late as she wishes in the morning, but call me as soon as she wakes," he commanded, not even glancing at Bess.

"Yes, my lord. Good night, my lord." With another curtsy she was gone.

He vaguely heard the door shut as he approached

Juliane's bedside. After gazing at her for a time, he blew out the candle beside her bed and said, "Good night, my angel, my . . ."

Adrian drew the hangings shut around the bed and pinched out the remaining candles. Leaving the room and going back to his own, he let the connecting doors remain open.

Easing himself between the fine lawn sheets which had been warmed, his mind whirled. He didn't realize he had gone to sleep until he heard the cries.

12

When the cries came again, he awoke with a start. Thinking he was in France, he reached for the dagger he usually kept with him. His panic at not finding it beside him brought him to full consciousness.

He was home—at Trees—why? Then the cries . . . ah! Adrian jumped up and, after fumbling briefly, found the flint and lit the candle. Shielding the flame with his hand, he ran to Lady Juliane's room. He jerked the bed draperies open and saw that she had been tossing wildly and was ensnarled in the bedding. Setting the candle down, he grabbed her shoulders and shook her. Her eyes flew open and at the wild fear and panic within them, Lord Adrian stepped back as if slapped.

"Juliane! Juliane. There is nothing to fear. It is I, Adrian."

She struggled fiercely, then collapsed back, closing her eyes.

Gently, he brushed the hair from her face, and eased her entanglement. "What is it? What is wrong?" He took her hand, clasping it tightly. Feeling the cold band of metal, he opened his hand and inspected the ring he found on her hand. It had a crest on it. Studying it closely, he memorized its features. It was his first clue as to who she was.

Lady Juliane moaned and began tossing about again.

"You are dreaming," he said soothingly. "A bad dream, but you are safe now."

She slowly opened her eyes and he saw that they were still glazed from the effects of the laudanum. It must have been a powerful dream to recall her to consciousness while under the drug's effect.

"Have they come back?" she asked, gripping his arm.

"Who, Juliane? Has who come back?"

"It is not enough that Judith is dead. Oh, God, she is dead." Tears ran down her cheeks.

Lord Adrian took her hands trying to comfort her. "Who is Judith?"

Juliane looked up at him pleadingly. "Why did they kill her? Why was the baron not there?"

"Baron? Who is the baron?"

"Thomas. I should have written Thomas. Why can I not find Uncle—why?" She was sobbing.

Sitting on the edge of the bed, he raised her and held her closely. Her arms tightened around him while she cried out all the grief and fear she had subdued since arriving at Rouen.

Holding Juliane, Lord Adrian felt his anger grow at whomever had caused her this pain.

A long while later he realized her sobbing had ceased; she had fallen asleep. Tenderly, he laid her back upon the pillows and straightened her covers. Softly, he placed a kiss upon her lips and, taking the candle, now nearly guttering out, walked slowly back into his room.

The sun's rays silhouetted the furniture. He dressed rapidly and, lighting a new candle, stalked from his room to the library in the main hall.

Holdt found him there later in the morning, poring over the latest registry of the aristocracy and gentry.

"What is it?" Lord Adrian asked brusquely.

"My lord, her ladyship wishes you to join her for breakfast."

"Tell her I will join her soon," he said absentmindedly. Closing the large book slowly, he stared into space. Things were certainly clearer. Was it relief he felt?

Perhaps Mother could be of some help, he thought, rising. Yes, she had always made it her business to know everyone elses'.

Adrian made a leg elegantly before Lady Tretain, then kissed her cheek. Sitting, he asked, "How are you this morning, Mother? I hope the journey did you no harm."

They sat in silence as Holdt served them and then withdrew at a wave of Lady Tretain's hand.

"The food is excellent, as usual, Mother. I do not know why I refrain from visiting. Perhaps I will come more frequently now."

"That you are finally considering taking your place

is good news indeed, my son. I thought you mentioned this was to be only a short visit."

"So I did. That is what this must be, but I mean to return, perhaps permanently, after only a brief time." He paused, then nonchalantly continued. "Mother—do you know anything of the Perrill family?"

Looking at him oddly, she asked, "Why do you ask?"

"Someone was mentioning them in London and I was curious. I do not recall having heard of them," he answered offhandedly.

"Well, let me think . . . the Perrills? I do believe I know of them. It seems the family title is earl . . . yes, I recall an Earl Lewallen. I think he went to his reward several years ago. They were not important. He depleted what remained of the family fortune at an early age," she finished scornfully.

"Do you know where the present earl is?"

"In India, I gather. I think there was a daughter who married a French nobleman—but it is too insignificant. I do not recall anything else. Let us speak of you, instead." She halted as Bess came shyly into the room.

A cold "Yes" greeted Bess's curtsy. "Begging your pardon, my lord, but you wished to be called when her ladyship awoke."

"Yes." He slapped his napkin onto the table and rose. "You must excuse me, Mother. I will speak with you later." Without further word, he strode from the room. Bess was forced into a half-run in order to keep up with him as he made his way through the hall, up the stairs, and to the master suites.

Knocking at Lady Juliane's door, he paused only to tell Bess to return when sent for.

"You vile creature," greeted him scathingly as he entered. "Where have you taken me? Where are the children? How could you?"

Adrian reached for her hand but she shrank from him. "Lady Perrill, there is no need for this."

Juliane gasped. How had he learned her name?

"You were quite talkative during the night under the effects of the laudanum," he said, in answer to her look.

"Laudanum. You odious man. I will . . ."

"You will what? I would think you could at least be more appreciative."

"Appreciative? I do not call being ruined something to thank one for, my lord."

"Who has been ruined?"

"You know I will never be able to appear in public once the rumours spread," she said accusingly.

"Why should there be any rumours?" he asked innocently.

"You are detestable."

"I am beginning to believe your education has been sadly neglected. Do you not know any complimentary terms?"

Lady Juliane folded her arms and glared.

Lord Adrian smiled back pleasantly. Seeing a comfortable chair near the fireplace, he moved it near the bed and seated himself.

"I demand you leave my room . . . and that I see the children."

"You may see the children as soon as we have completed our conversation."

"I have none to make with you, my lord."

"You are wrong there, my dear." Pursing his lips, he added, "Do you not think it rather odd to call me 'my lord' after a marriage of such long 'duration'? He caught the pillow she hurled at him and smoothed it on his lap. "If you must treat me as a husband, the least you can do is call me by name. Mother will think it decidedly odd if you do not."

"Mother? We are not at . . ."

"Trees, my dear. You surely can remember our country estate. But, of course, the illness has affected your memory severely. I must remember to tell the servants that," he said smoothly.

"What illness? I will not be here long enough for you to tell anyone anything."

"You are wrong, Juliane. If you insist on being disagreeable, I will merely imply you still are not well. Your having arrived here in a state of unconsciousness will lend credence to my tale and, of course, Mallatt will agree entirely with me."

Shaking her head, she asked tiredly, "Why? Why are you doing this?"

They gazed at each other steadily. It was Lady Juliane who dropped her eyes first; Lord Adrian's were no longer cool. When she looked up, the mask was back.

"Let us say I dislike anyone who seeks to harm an innocent child. Can you not trust me and tell me the whole?" he asked earnestly.

"I am so glad to see you recovered, child," said Lady Tretain as she unexpectedly entered and moved to the center of the room.

Ignoring the chilling stare from her son, she continued, "I have ordered your breakfast, and I thought you both would be desirous of knowing that I have decided that a ball shall be held in your honour, a score of days hence."

"A ball," came the stunned reply in unison.

"Mother, have you gone daft?" stated Lord Adrian.

"Of course not, my son. I merely wish to give . . . Lady Tretain the . . . the proper welcome and introduction. Everyone will be agog to learn who has snared you at last. A fortnight should allow you ample time to arrange for proper dress to be sent from London. Satter tells me your wife's wardrobe is most . . . inadequate."

So, thought Lord Adrian glowering, the gauntlet is thrown. Well, his mother would not win so easily. He relaxed, forcing a smile. "How . . . kind . . . of you, Mother. We are suitably honoured, are we not, Juliane?"

Lady Juliane looked from mother to son. Why, one was as daft as the other.

13

The day was touched with a hint of spring. A carefree week had sped by, the only reminder of fear being the two men that watched over Lady Juliane and the children by day, and another two who stood guard at the children's door by night.

When not busy with affairs of the estate, Lord Adrian went out of his way to find amusement for Lady Juliane, often including the children. This was to Juliane's delight and Lady Tretain's continuing astonishment.

Lady Tretain had decided to be coldly pleasant. Since Lady Juliane was accustomed to such treatment in India, it bothered her little. Her reaction unknowingly raised her esteem in the eyes of Lady Tretain. Although hesitant to accept Lady Juliane because of the suspicious circumstances surrounding her advent into the family, Lady Tretain reluctantly admitted that the change wrought by Juliane in her son was short of miraculous.

Instead of brooding by day and thundering who knew where by night, as he had on past visits, he went about with a festive spirit, enticing others to laugh. She had never seen him happier, and yet a nagging apprehension haunted her. She could not believe he was, in fact, married or that the children were his. If it was as she believed, it could only end in disaster.

She could find no fault with the children. They were lovable. If only she could be at ease. If Adrian did indeed call her bluff and go through with the ball, she would have to admit defeat at her own hand.

The warmth of the air and the golden splash of crocuses on the sculptured lawn had enticed Lady Juliane and the children outdoors. She was enjoying a most unladylike romp when Lord Adrian approached carrying an oversized wicker basket.

André ran to greet him and even Leora toddled toward him. Catching her small hand in his, he led them back to where Lady Juliane was seated on the ground.

Under his scrutinizing gaze she became conscious of her disheveled appearance. Brushing leaves and dried grass from her hair and gown, she began to rise.

"No, my lady. I will join you if I may."

"What did you bring us, *mon père*?" squealed André.

"You must wait. Leora," he took her fingers and

drew her to his lap as he knelt beside Lady Juliane. "I trust this is safe?" he asked in mock seriousness.

Juliane smiled broadly. "I believe so, my lord, but one can never be certain."

"I will risk it; am I not *courageux*, André?"

André giggled in return. This "papa" was so foolish at times.

Holding onto Leora, Lord Adrian pulled the basket closer. André knelt beside them. The anticipation lighting the children's faces infected Lady Juliane.

"Open the lid, Leora," coaxed Lord Adrian.

Lady Juliane and André watched in expectation as her tiny fingers fumbled with the lid. Curious squeaks, squeals, and something suspiciously close to a meow coming from the basket became too much for André. He reached across and lifted the lid.

A large black mongrel pup tumbled out and pounced into Lady Juliane's lap, nipping at her skirts. Then, a small black kitten placed its paws on the edge of the basket and peered cautiously over the brim.

Laughing, Lady Juliane fended off the puppy's face-washing efforts and handed the bundle of energy to André. The pair was soon becoming very well acquainted, chasing one another and rolling in the grass.

Lord Adrian removed the kitten from the basket and, holding it in one hand, guided Leora's hand over the silky fur.

Looking across at Juliane, he hesitated briefly, then said, "Your gift should be here tomorrow—two days hence at latest."

The laughter died in her eyes, and looking down,

she plucked at the dry grass. "You know I cannot accept a gift from you, my lord," she said. "I should not allow your kindness to these children; it will but make things more difficult for them later."

"Then let us not term it a gift but a payment. I am responsible . . ." He halted at the look of dismay on her face.

"Here is Alva—it is time for the children to go in," said Juliane, rising.

Lord Adrian rose also, and handed Leora to Alva. "André will come in later," he said. "Let him play with his pup for a time."

"Aye, m'lord," Alva said.

Lady Juliane frowned.

"Do not be angry with me. Surely you had a pup or pet of some sort at his age. I remember . . ."

"Yes, I know," she interrupted, remembering the grief he had expressed in his delirium.

"Will you not walk with me until André tires?" Adrian asked, sensing her change in mood.

She searched for a reason to decline but, finding none that was reasonable, said, "Yes, my lord."

He took her arm. "I think you will enjoy the gardens. I know they will give you much enjoyment later this season when the roses are in bloom."

"You know that will be impossible, my lord. I must leave soon."

"You cannot."

"Why? You do not mean to go through with the ball?" she asked, searching his face.

"I do not know. But I cannot permit you to go just yet."

"You cannot permit?" she echoed indignantly.

"We have been at peace for a week now. Why is it we must cross swords whenever we are alone?" asked Lord Adrian wearily.

"Because you insist on this pretense. More than harming me, it is unjust to the children. They are unsettled enough as it is, but this constant shifting of attention and emotions can only do them ill. The gifts you have just given them reinforce the idea of a father that cannot be."

"Why can it not be?" He halted and looked intently into her eyes. "You still cannot place your faith in me?"

Lady Juliane read the regret on his features but could not answer him. She walked on.

Lord Adrian followed, shouting a greeting to a gardener in the distance. They continued in silence, each absorbed in private thought.

As they were turning to come back, they heard a shrill whistle. Ahead of them, near a copse, André and the pup were romping.

The whistle sounded again and the pup sat and perked up his ears. At the next sound of the whistle, he bounded into the copse, André following. His bodyguard watched unconcerned.

When André did not emerge, Lady Juliane increased her step and called to him. She was answered with a scream from within. All of her old fears filled her anew, and, picking up her skirts, she raced for the copse.

The bodyguard and Lord Adrian entered the thicket first. Lady Juliane struggled to follow them as the branches tore at her gown.

"André! André!" she called, but there was no answer.

Continuing on, she lost sight of Lord Adrian and the bodyguard but she could hear the crunch of gravel and the snap of branches about her. Would there never be a clearing? Then, coming to a small one, she tripped and half fell. Looking down, she saw she had tripped on a large rock; picking it up, she pressed forward.

Meanwhile André was kicking and thrashing with all his might. His abductor, hampered by the closeness of the trees and brush, loosened his grip momentarily.

"Ma mère!" screamed André.

As the hand closed over his mouth once more, André sunk his teeth into it and the man let loose a stream of curses.

Hearing this, Lady Juliane realized she was near them. She pushed on with all her strength. An explosive snap to the right drew her. Yes, she could see a man—and he had André.

Holding her skirts tightly with one hand, she edged forward. Coming within reach, she dropped her skirts and raised the rock with both hands. As the man turned at her sound, she brought it down. He crumpled, senseless, to the ground and André writhed free and flew to Juliane.

As she held him tightly, she looked at the prone figure in horror; blood was oozing through his hair and dripping to the ground.

Snapping and crackling brought Lady Juliane's head around and she saw Lord Adrian and the bodyguard close behind him. Instead of being relieved at the sight of them, Lord Adrian looked angry.

Kneeling, Lord Adrian placed a hand over the man's heart. "He's alive. Morton, take this scoundrel and lock him up. I will question him later. Juliane, are you and André unharmed?"

"Yes, my lord."

He was struck by her coldness.

"Let me take you back to the house. We must be doubly careful in the future. If I am to help you, you must tell me what this is about."

"I will think on it, my lord," she answered as they came into the open. Suspicion formed a cold ring about her heart. Was it he they had to fear? What could he gain? There was so much they did not know about him and she had come so close to entrusting him with their safety.

She could not discount, however much she wished to, that the attempt had been made only after she had failed to agree that they go on in the current manner. Had Lord Adrian's greeting to the gardener really been a signal to proceed with the kidnapping?

The situation was becoming increasingly confusing. It seemed she was surrounded by enemies. But why? What did they want?

14

Lady Tretain kept a studied eye on Lady Juliane, while trying to assume an engrossed pose over her needlework.

It had been a week since the attempt to abduct André, with the captured man's escape occurring that same night, and she still had been unable to learn the reason for the kidnapping.

Since that time, she had also noticed that, although her son continued his carefree manner with Lady Juliane, her careful restraint toward him had definitely taken an icy turn. If Lord Adrian had noticed, he was letting no one know, despite the sharp words that had occurred over the escape. It was as though Lady Juliane thought Adrian had set the man free.

For the first time since their arrival at Trees, Lord Adrian had failed to join them for the evening meal. Although this had upset Lady Tretain, Lady Juliane was more relieved than distressed. She did not feel prepared for the confrontation, which she felt certain would ensue over the voluminous stack of boxes and packages that had been delivered to her room that day from London—Adrian's promised gift.

She had declined to open even one, certain of what was within, and their presence in her room strengthened her resolve to leave Trees as quickly as she could fathom a method.

"Lady Juliane, are you listening?"

"Pardon, my lady, my mind was wandering. What is it you were saying?"

"Arrangements for the ball are complete. Preparations will begin on the morrow. I have received confirmation from all of those invited and Lord and Lady Stern will be arriving the day after the morrow, also. Of course, Sir Percival Elliott, my husband's nephew, is coming and Adrian has indicated some of his friends will join us." Seeing that this statement had somehow upset Lady Juliane, Lady Tretain asked, "Was there someone you wished to invite?"

"No, I can think of no one," she faltered.

It would soon be too late. Once visitors arrived, her chance to escape would be gone. Adrian had to tell the truth, they could not go through with this. What did he hope to accomplish?

"As I was saying, my dear, the decorations will be in Lord Adrian's favourite colours, silver and blue. He has said the gown he ordered for you is in those colours; do you wish to go through the family jewels? I am certain you will find something among them to complement your gown."

"I am sorry, Lady Tretain. What is it you were saying?" she asked, giving her head a shake as if to clear it.

"Nothing, Lady Juliane. Perhaps it would be best if we retired for the evening."

"Yes," Lady Juliane answered absentmindedly, "I believe so." She laid down the needlework that had remained untouched.

"May I ask, is all well with you?" Lady Tretain inquired, thawing briefly.

"Yes. Everything is as it has been. I bid you goodnight."

Up in her room, Lady Juliane paced. The two bodyguards were on duty outside the children's rooms. Once they had seemed to lend security; now they were a hindrance. How could she manage to get away without them knowing?

A new thought struck her: had Lord Adrian placed them there to keep an abductor out or to keep the children in? She must have this out with him.

Bess entered quietly. "Will you be wishing to retire now, my lady, or shall I return later?"

"You may retire now, Bess. I will look after myself." She waved away Bess's protests. "I am more accustomed to doing for myself than you would guess. Be on your way. Good night."

There has to be a way out, she thought. This is not a prison. Lord Adrian seems to desire to please me in all things, for whatever good it does him. Mayhap I can use this. If only I could dispense with the guards. Yes, I have it. There will be no need to speak with him. Now for a good night's rest. I will need it.

Juliane soon fell into a fitful sleep. Hounded by dreams of disaster, she twisted and turned. The dream became reality as she realized the hand upon her shoulder was not imagination. Her scream was stifled by a firm hand.

"Calm yourself, there is nothing to fear. I must speak with you," Lord Adrian said urgently.

She stared at the figure before her. His hair was windswept and his breeches and boots mud-stained. In the candlelight there was something frightening in his pose.

She pulled the covers higher, "What is it you want?"

Smiling ruefully at her action, he relaxed imperceptibly and sat on the bed. "I am sorry to frighten you in this way, but Mallatt has told me that guests will be arriving two days hence. We must be in agreement on several points before they reach Trees."

"I see no need, my lord . . ."

"When will you end this pretense?" He gripped her arm. "You have no choice but to do as I command."

"No one commands me," she said, attempting to wrench her hand free.

Capturing both her hands and holding them painfully, he hissed, "You will obey me."

Lady Juliane stemmed her anger, recalling her plans for the morrow, and choked out a weak, "Yes, my lord."

Lord Adrian froze at this unexpected answer. He had fully expected a major row. "I am glad you have come to your senses at last; it will ease things for both of us.

"When Lord and Lady Stern and our other visitors arrive, you will answer their questions truthfully, to an extent. At all times, be vague as to the length of our marriage. Simply ignore questions concerning the children. The only facts we will be open about is that you have been in France with the children and we will reveal your family name."

"But, my lord," she said, forgetting herself momentarily, "that would leave me open to all manner of questions and," she added bitterly, "ensure my downfall."

"Never fear for that, I have my plans. Did the garments I ordered arrive?"

"Yes, my lord," she answered tartly.

"Were they satisfactory?"

"But what else, my lord," she snapped. "If that is all you wish, I would like to return to sleep."

Something in her voice disturbed him. She had not quibbled or refused the garments. Something was amiss. This decided him against telling her of the progress being made in locating the abductors—the reason for his being absent.

"I bid you good night then, my lady. Sleep well." Taking the candle and turning to leave, his eye caught the neatly stacked boxes and parcels in the shadows of the far corner of the room. Shifting back to Lady Juliane, he asked, "We are in agreement then?"

"Of course, my lord. As you say, I have little choice."

Juliane watched as the door closed after his retreating figure. "I must be successful tomorrow, for my sake as well as the children's!"

15

The morning brought heart-sinking disappointment to Lady Juliane. Her plans were of no use, as the weather was completely uncooperative.

She stood gazing out of the floor-length windows which graced the outer wall of the smaller family salon. The rain was pelting mercilessly against them and the wind swept savagely through the budding branches of the trees. There would be no venturing outdoors this day.

Lady Juliane did not know anyone had entered the room until she heard, near her shoulder, "Such weather is depressing, is it not?"

Starting at the unexpected intrusion, she drew in a breath as she turned her head and saw Lord Adrian at her side. She relaxed slightly as she realized he could not read her thoughts.

Adrian watched the play of emotions on her fea-

tures and stifled a smile as she assumed an unconcerned air.

"It is just that I had planned an outing for the
children today, my lord. I had not told them, so they
are spared the disappointment, but I had looked forward to it."

"I dislike seeing you disappointed," Lord Adrian
said. "And for a fact your time with the children will
be considerably lessened once our house guests begin
to arrive on the morrow. I have an idea—you shall
have your outing."

"In this weather? It is impossible."

"We need not go outdoors for an outing. You will
see. Bring the children to this room for their
luncheon." He smiled conspiratorially.

"As you wish, my lord," she answered carelessly.

"Come, can you not show more interest than this?"
he asked with an injured air. Would his attempts to
win her approval never succeed?

Lady Juliane paused. It was difficult to determine
whether his injured expression was sincere or just
more of his usual mockery. "I am sorry to appear un-
grateful, my lord," she said tiredly, "but you realize
fully I do not wish to continue this deception."

"Do not tell the children anything," he said, ignoring her words.

"As you wish, my lord." She turned back to the
window. There was a long silence and then she heard
the doors close.

Sinking into one of the chairs near the fireplace,
she had the uncommon urge to cry. What was wrong
with her these days? Why should Lord Adrian have
such an unsettling effect on her?

André bubbled over with questions when Lady Juliane led him and Leora from their rooms to the small salon in which they were to have their "outing." They paused as Holdt opened the doors.

"Hurry—come in," called Lord Adrian.

The children rushed in; Lady Juliane followed more slowly. The sight which confronted them made them halt in their steps.

Lord Adrian had managed to assemble a miniature farm scene. Green boughs from cedars and pines, and flowers from the estate's greenhouses gave a breath of spring and openness to the room. A small flock of chicks and ducks was scurrying about. A tiny lamb nuzzled Leora, who responded with a tentative pat, then sunk both hands and face into its soft wool, babbling happily.

André's puppy bounded atop him and they fell into a happy heap upon the floor. Lady Juliane could only shake her head in wonder. What had put such an idea into his head?

"Do you approve, Juliane?" he asked, taking her hand and leading her before a large cloth spread before the fire. It was laden with all the ingredients necessary for an outdoor feast. Several large pillows had been placed around the cloth.

"May I assist you?" Lord Adrian asked, nodding at the pillows.

She inclined her head and he took her hands as she lowered herself to one of the pillows. He held them longer than was strictly necessary. Glancing up, her breath caught at the look in his eyes. Doubts fled as she felt a warm flame come to life within her breast.

His lips brushed her inner wrist, causing her pulse to leap wildly.

Adrian raised his eyes to hers. The children, their surroundings, all was forgotten in the silent burst of emotion enveloping them. Their gazes held with a spellbinding force until urgent tugs from the children forced them to part.

Leora was pulling at Juliane's gown and André was yanking at Lord Adrian's coat.

Releasing Juliane's hand and sighing with regret, Lord Adrian picked up André and tossed him in the air. "What is it, *mon fin compagnon?*"

"We are *affamé*—can we not eat?" demanded André.

"You will have to wait to eat, André," laughed Lady Juliane. "Leora has 'requested' a certain change be made first."

Seeing the puddle beneath Leora's feet, Lord Adrian burst into laughter. "You see to the change, Juliane—I shall see to 'repairs' here. Hurry though— you have two hungry bears waiting."

"*Oui,*" echoed André, "hurry."

Returning shortly, Lady Juliane and Leora entered to find Lord Adrian and André seated upon the cushions. André made a guilty swallow and grinned. Leora ran on tiptoes and plopped down on a pillow beside them.

Lord Adrian rose, bowed exaggeratedly to Lady Juliane, and seated her. Shaking out a napkin, he draped it across her lap.

Laughing at his manner, she said, "No, my lord, you must not. I shall serve myself."

He bowed so low that even André laughed. Startled, Leora looked about. Lord Adrian plucked her up and tossed her into the air. Her alarm was followed by enthusiastic jabbering.

André was up in an instant, begging for the same. Lowering Leora, Lord Adrian swung André up, then, pretending he was about to drop him, staggered about and collapsed on the cushions. The salon resounded with their gaiety.

Servants passing the salon's closed doors for the next hour smiled at the sound of the laughter. It was good, indeed, to have the master home and the house full of the sounds of happiness.

Alva lifted a weary Leora to her shoulder.

"André, you must go also," admonished Lord Adrian as André backed from Alva's outstretched hand. "We will have more outings."

"Do you promise?" sniffed André.

"I give you my promise as a gentleman," he answered, taking André by the hand and leading him to Alva. "And you know a gentleman always keeps his word. Now off with you." Giving the boy a pat, he held the door as Alva and the children passed through. As they left, he turned and approached Lady Juliane, who had risen. "There is still some time before we have to dress for dinner. Come with me." Taking her hand, he led her from the salon.

"Holdt," he called, "see to the menagerie in the salon and tell all those concerned that it was an unmitigated success."

"Yes, my lord. I will be most pleased to do so."

"We are going to the library—see that we are NOT interrupted."

"Yes, my lord."

In the library Lady Juliane edged closer to her corner as Lord Adrian seated himself beside her on the small sofa before the fire. She had been so completely at ease with him during their "outing" that she had forgotten her fears and plans. Looking at him as he gazed into the fire, seriousness changing him, her anxiety returned.

A low sigh escaped Lord Adrian. Leaning back, he placed his arm atop the sofa, half encircling Lady Juliane. "You enjoyed the afternoon."

It was a statement, not a question, but she felt impelled to reply. "It was delightful, my lord. I must thank you—for the children." Her brow wrinkled slightly.

"But, something troubled you about it?" he asked quietly.

"No, my lord. It could not have been improved upon. It is just." She hesitated, then honesty gained the upper hand. She looked away and continued, "I do wish you had not given your promise to André."

"But it is a promise easily kept."

Lady Juliane wrung her hands; it was so disquieting, having him so near. Would her heart not be still?

Adrian placed his strong, slim hand atop hers firmly, and she turned to him. His gaze caused her heart to race and, as he leaned closer, all her fears left. He paused, his eyes searching hers.

Juliane read the ardent question in them, and felt

an ensuing tumult within her heart. All of her carefully nourished reservations were pushed aside.

Slowly Adrian brushed a tendril from her cheek. His touch brought a flush to her cheeks. I must not let myself be drawn to this man, she thought, even as she felt herself yield to the hand drawing her to him. Their lips brushed lightly. Juliane drew back—one last question had to be asked before she surrendered to the emotion pulsing through her being.

"What, my angel?" Adrian asked with velvet gentleness, his desire tightly reined.

Just as she opened her mouth to ask, the library doors were thrown open.

Lord Adrian was on his feet instantly, a low "Damnation!" coming from his lips as he turned. Lady Juliane felt she had been set adrift in a sea of confusion with no lifeline near. Had she been saved, or had her chance for true happiness been lost?

Lord Adrian's shout of joy at the sight of the elegant gentleman entering was lost upon her, but the answering reply was not; it was French.

Her confusion was suddenly replaced by fear and uncertainty as she rose to confront the two men gazing at her.

"Ah, I can see why you were not to be disturbed, *mon ami*. Most decidedly." He made a leg elegantly, moving his lace-covered hands in gallant acknowledgment of Lady Juliane.

"My dear, may I present Louís Joseph Marie Coceau, Count de Cavilón."

She curtsied appropriately.

"Louís, my wife, Lady Juliane."

Lady Juliane glanced sharply at his tone, and

153

turned from his look. One would have thought he had just introduced a woman whom he was proud and happy to call his wife.

How skillful he is, she thought, hardening her heart. He is more dangerous than I imagined. No, she amended sadly. It is your heart that threatens betrayal. "If you will excuse me, my lords, I must retire to dress for dinner." She needed solitude to gain a firmer grip on her emotions.

"Of course, Juliane," replied Lord Adrian, taking her hand and leading her to the door. "I have instructed Bess as to which gown I wish you to wear this evening, and I will come to escort you to dinner personally," he added so only she could hear.

Failing to fathom his look, she glanced beyond him. "My lord," she said, nodding to the count as she left.

Lord Adrian watched her briefly, then turned back to his friend and cryptically uttered, "Must you always have such abominable timing? One would think you Frenchmen know nothing of love."

The count puzzled over this, then laughed. "I received your most urgent summons, bid farewell to my most promising 'friend', and traveled in the most damnable weather, only to be told when I arrive that you are with your 'family' and cannot be disturbed. *Naturellement* I was happy to be given occasion to make myself presentable, but to be kept waiting for an hour by an *épouse*?" He cocked his head questioningly.

"I did not think you would ever marry, *mon ami*. Do you not recall the time I discovered you in that little inn in Riems pretending to be a cleric? I had decided that was more than a *masque*."

Tretain grinned wryly. "Is that why you told the young lady there that I was *dément?*"

"How could I know you wished to hear her *confession?*" Cavilón asked as he sat with exaggerated delicacy. "So *frauduleux,*" he smiled.

"But effective—no thanks to you."

"If I recall correctly, you were able to get your proof against Monsieur Refand. Has he had opportunity to sell more English military plans since then? But you know," Cavilón continued, waving aside the obvious reply, "your disguise as a *chevalier* shortly after that must have been vastly more entertaining. That time I was no hindrance."

"No," Tretain smiled warmly at his friend. "Without you my life would have been forfeit, for they had grown suspicious. But that was long ago," he shrugged the reminiscence aside. "I was very green then."

"Your government did not value you highly enough, Adrian, to have used you so dangerously.

"They had to know if that villain the Comte de Pauleux was using his connections to pass on false information. The treaty for the Peace of Paris was being drafted. . . . But that was ten years past. The comte was not successful—neither was the treaty," he ended wryly.

"*Non,*" Cavilón agreed. "And you continue in your dangerous ways. Lord Palmer told me of your recent journey to France and how fruitful it was. You not only learned the direction of the army and its generals' intent, but spirited Lord Evansly to freedom as well. I congratulate you, *mon ami.*" He eyed his friend steadily.

"You forget Arblay." Adrian's lips had tightened into a thin line. "I was not able to secure his safety."

Cavilón shrugged. "Yes, a regrettable loss but unavoidable in the circumstances. You betrayed nothing and nearly lost your life as well."

"Arblay did lose his." Tretain shook his head. "But what of you? With the king executed . . ."

"We dwell on unpleasant matters . . . most *désegréable*," the count dismissed the earl's words. "Tell me, how have you reconciled this 'work' you do for the government with your wife?"

"She knows nothing of it," Tretain answered curtly. "Since Palmer now has you in his toils—do not deny it, it is the only way you could have learned as much as you did—" he continued lightly "—there may be no need for my services in the future. Let us speak no more on it—I have a more serious matter to discuss. Come, I will explain as I dress."

Lady Juliane seethed as she paced. Bess was close to tears. She could not understand what had so upset her ladyship; why, one would think she was angry at his lordship, and how could that be? After all, the gowns, undergarments, and accessories were the finest and most beautiful one could imagine. She had thought it an added touch of kindness that his lordship had ordered the unpacking; he had explained that Lady Juliane was much too busy to see to it. So why this tantrum. They had said downstairs that one could never understand the Quality and at this moment she was ready to agree.

"Oh, that scheming, abominable man," Lady Juliane muttered. She had been discomposed ever since

Bess had raised the green, watered-silk gown and held it for her to see.

All of the boxes and packets had disappeared. She had stalked to the wardrobe, thrown open the doors, and gasped at the array of colours and materials within. Looking closer, her jaw tightened; all of her practical, serviceable gowns had been removed. "Of all the loathesome things to do," she said to herself while pacing. "He could charm a snake out of his skin and the snake wouldn't know it."

The sound of laughter echoed through the connecting passageway into her room. In a burst of unusual temper, she grabbed the figurine on a table close at hand and threw it at the offending sound.

The figurine, predictably shattering against the door, stilled the laughter and a few moments later, Lord Adrian, in breeches and open-necked shirt, cautiously opened the door.

"Is something troubling you, my lady?" he asked in vexatious innocence.

Through clenched teeth, Lady Juliane forced herself to say, "No, my lord. An accident merely."

"You have not yet begun to dress," he said accusingly. "There is only a short time before we must go down." He turned to go back to his room. "Your eyes are most beautiful." Reading her response, he judiciously hastened to close the door behind him.

Lady Juliane started toward the doorway to the hall, but the sight of Bess stopped her. She would not add to the gossip, certain that enough had already been gathered from the scene.

Just once, she thought, I would dearly love putting him in his place. Capitulating for the moment, she allowed Bess to assist her in arraying herself in the garments Lord Adrian had provided. Having to concede that his taste was impeccable, if a bit extravagant, only increased her anger. When Bess had completed the finishing touches, she refused to look at her reflection in the mirror, but seated herself primly and awaited his lordship.

Rising at his knock, she motioned for Bess to open the door. Lord Adrian halted when he saw her, a smile of deep satisfaction on his features. "Lovely, my dear, you are as I imagined, a statuesque Greek goddess. These should suit admirably." He held out a velvet-covered box.

Lady Juliane refused to take it, her eyes conveying a volume of unspoken feelings.

Lord Adrian opened the box and handed it to Bess. He removed a delicate gold chain set with emeralds. Standing close behind Juliane, he fastened it about her neck and placed a matching bracelet upon her wrist.

At his touch, her anger had turned to something quite different, and she allowed him to place her hand upon his arm as they went to the hall.

Late that night, Juliane raised her head from a tear-soaked pillow, sat up in the darkness, and wiped her eyes with the edge of the sheet. You are being exceedingly missish, she reprimanded herself, and you know you cannot tolerate missish women. This pronouncement threatened to induce a fresh bout of weeping.

Foolish woman, she thought, wasting all this energy over yourself, when it is the children you should be concerned with. Sadly, she had to admit that from the moment she and Lord Adrian had entered the library that afternoon, she had entirely forgotten the children. He filled her thoughts completely. His touch—his nearness—sent her heart singing.

Sighing, she hugged her knees to her comfortingly. I must concentrate on the children. She sighed once more. Tomorrow I must go through with my plan before it is too late.

Reassured by her thoughts, but realizing her emotions were far too close to betraying the love she refused to recognize, Juliane fell into an uneasy sleep.

16

Bright rays of the sun were reflected from the dew-covered lawn, creating a carpet of sparkling diamonds shimmering with the promise of an excellent day.

Lady Juliane had been down to breakfast early, thereby escaping an encounter with anyone. She instructed Holdt to have a small landau ready by mid-morning and to have the cook prepare a picnic luncheon. After ordering the luncheon placed in the landau and another wicker basket sent to her room, she went to the temporary nursery.

Alva was dressing André and the servant assigned to help her was just finishing with Leora.

Taking Leora, Lady Juliane dismissed the servant girl. "We are going for an outing this morning, Alva. It is such a pleasant day for one. It should be warm enough by mid-morning for just light jackets—but bring along the children's heavy wraps."

Handing Leora to Alva, she said, "Take them into

the other room for breakfast. Have them ready by mid-morning. I will come for you."

"Yes, m'lady. Be something wrong?" asked Alva, hesitating at the door.

"No, of course not—go on." Juliane waited until Alva and the children were gone. Then, going to the wardrobe, she searched through it and removed several sets of the children's clothing. Coming out of the room, she assumed her most nonchalant air as she walked across the hall with her armful of clothing, ignoring the questioning looks of the watchful guards.

Once in her room, she packed the children's garments and added a few of her own things she had located. She had found it necessary to include a few of the new undergarments but was determined, even if it necessitated hardship, that she would not take any of the new gowns. Her packing finished, she went in search of Holdt.

The house was a hive of activity as servants worked to ready the huge ballroom and prepare the guest rooms. Lady Juliane was hopeful that all this activity would divert everyone's attention from her clandestine activities.

Locating Holdt, she ordered the landau to be left near the stables instead of brought to the house, offering the children's desire to see Lord Adrian's animals as an excuse.

Lady Tretain collared her as she made her way toward the stairs. "Come, my dear, see how well preparations are proceeding. From this evening on until the guests depart, I shall send Satter to do your hair." She frowned. "We cannot have it seen as such."

As Lady Juliane was planning on not being present

this evening, she thanked Lady Tretain for her kindness and allowed her to lead the way into the ballroom.

"This is the first time this room will be used since my husband's death." To Juliane's surprise a fleeting sorrow passed over her features. "Do you approve?"

Looking about, Lady Juliane felt a twinge of sadness—it would have been wonderful to reign over such a splendid room.

A myriad of servants were busy polishing the oak wainscoting and the floor to mirror perfection. Others were polishing the score of huge candelabra placed along the walls and filling them with fresh candles. Elegant bouquets of flowers made from blue and silver lamé were still being constructed.

"It is most beautiful, Lady Tretain," Lady Juliane answered sincerely.

"I am glad you feel so. I must go now—so much to see to. I will see you at luncheon."

"No, I will not be there," Lady Juliane fidgeted. "I am taking the children on a picnic—my last chance to do so and the weather is so glorious this morning."

"But, I thought Lord Adrian . . . well, never mind. Enjoy yourselves." With a wave of her hand she was off.

Lady Juliane hurried back to her room and took up her cloak. It was time to be off. Going into the nursery, she helped Alva button up the children, procured the wicker basket from her bed, and picked up Leora. In the hall, Juliane smiled at the two men assigned to guard them. Best to seem natural so they would not become suspicious. Alva rejoined the group and they made their way to the stableyard where the landau awaited.

Motioning for Alva to put the basket under the seat of the landau, Juliane turned to one of the guards. "I have forgotten my umbrella. Would you be so kind as to fetch it? You will find it on my bed."

When he was out of hearing, she had Alva hand André into the carriage. After Alva had followed him, she handed Leora to her.

"Oh, I had forgotten—Holdt desired a word with you," she said to the remaining guard. "In one of the greenhouses, I believe. We will wait for you. No one can harm us here."

The man frowned but, not daring to disobey, went on his way. Heartened by her success thus far, Lady Juliane dismissed the driver and ordered him to hand her up.

"But you cannot mean to drive off alone, my lady," the groom exclaimed when he realized her intent.

"We are not going far. Lord Adrian knows of this. Do not worry. Now, release their heads."

The groom did so reluctantly and watched them out of sight. "That be odd," he said to the driver, "but, if his lordship knows, who are we to disagree?"

The crunch of the chipped gravel beneath the hooves and wheels sung a song of freedom to Lady Juliane. She had hoped for a livelier pair than those before her, but they would do. Drawing out of sight of the house, her assurance of success grew.

The path they followed led them through a wooded area and after the brilliant sunshine the filtered murkiness cast a pall on their spirits.

"Be ye certain of where we be goin'?" asked Alva, glancing about. The children seemed to draw on her mood as they huddled closer.

"Of course. Now smile—why such a lowering look?"

"I have a feelin', m'lady, and it bodes no good," answered Alva with increasing nervousness.

Even the horses sensed something afoot and became restive in their paces.

Lady Juliane forced herself to remain calm. Once we are out of the woods, she assured herself, this feeling will evaporate. "Come, children, let us sing a song," she said, leading them in a familiar French nursery tune.

Alva joined in as best she could and their spirits brightened somewhat, until they realized they were not alone in their singing. One by one, they became silent with Lady Juliane trailing off last, her heart sinking. The song still surrounded them.

Flipping the reins, Lady Juliane admonished Alva to hold onto Leora and for André to find a grip. As the horses increased their gait, the muffled sound of hooves drowned out the nursery tune.

Casting a look back, Lady Juliane spied four horses following. She could not see their riders. The whip came into her hand and she applied it vigourously. Even with this, the horsemen drew closer.

"They be masked," screamed Alva, clutching Leora. "Lord above, save us!"

Closer still they drew; there seemed no escape.

Hurtling into the bright sunshine with the riders in close pursuit, Lady Juliane caught a glimpse of movement to her right. She was too fully occupied with the horses to think on it.

One of the riders had gained her pair's heads and was reaching for the bridle. Lady Juliane struck at him fruitlessly with the whip, using some of the more expressive phrases she had heard used by her brother's men in India.

Her momentary feeling of success was shattered by a volley of gunshots.

As the four riders made for the forest, Mallatt, leading a group of grooms with fowling pieces, pursued. Lord Adrian and Count Cavilón raced after the still speeding landau.

Lady Juliane's gratitude at being rescued diminished when she recognized her deliverers. As Lord Adrian and the count brought the horses to a halt, her lips became a thin line.

Turning their horses back to the occupants of the landau, Lord Adrian smiled grimly while Count Cavilón maintained a blank demeanour.

"That was *magnifique*," cried André, standing. Alva and Leora were crying—Alva from fright and relief, Leora from being held in a crushing grip.

Lady Juliane sat ramrod straight, unspeaking.

"How careless of my men to leave you unattended. I must discipline them."

"That will not be necessary," said Lady Juliane quietly, mindful of the count's scrutinizing gaze.

"Truly," quipped Lord Adrian. "I hear you are destined for a picnic. Knowing Cook, she will have prepared enough food for a batallion. We will join you." He dismounted, tied his mount to the rear of the landau, and climbed up, seating himself beside Lady Juliane.

165

She refused to look at him even when he took the reins.

"May I compliment you on your command of the English language, my dear," Lord Adrian said languidly, flicking the horses into motion. "We could not hear you clearly, of course, but your education does seem to be diverse."

Lady Juliane's blush rose higher, but still she refused to rise to the bait.

Reaching a clump of pines, Lord Adrian halted the team. He stepped down and reached up to assist Lady Juliane. Ungraciously, she allowed him to do so.

Alva shook her head in puzzlement at the black look of Lady Juliane as she reached for Leora.

"I had no idea you were so fond of outings, Juliane," noted Lord Adrian, taking the wicker basket from beneath Alva's feet.

Lady Juliane bit her lip—that was not the basket of food. "My lord," she said, concentrating on Leora's jacket, "I have . . . have forgotten to thank you. Let me do so by serving your lunch. If you will but give the basket to me?" She looked at him as guilelessly as she could.

"I would not think of it, my dear," he assured her. "I am certain this 'luncheon' will be sufficient reward."

"But, no, my lord. Take Leora for me."

Lord Adrian balanced the basket atop the wheel. "Is there something troubling you?"

"I—" she stammered, "I—that is, that is the wrong basket, my lord. It contains . . . extra clothing for the children," she finished lamely.

Lord Adrian raised the edge of the basket lid.

Reaching inside, he raised a lace chemise just high enough for Lady Juliane to see. "Do you not think Leora a bit young for this?" he asked with raised eyebrow.

Blushing fiercely, Lady Juliane reached across and slammed the lid shut, barely missing Lord Adrian's hand.

"I am most fortunate you are so good-natured," he smiled, putting the basket back and removing the other.

17

"Success" was not the word Lady Juliane would have used to describe her "outing." A day after the fact she still fumed over it, not so much that she had failed, but that she was forced to endure Lord Adrian and Count Cavilón's idle chatter the entire afternoon. If only he had mentioned something, anything, about her attempted escape, but, no, the pompous buck had pressed on as if nothing had happened. Compounding matters, André adored him even more. What was she to do?

Even worse was the role she had to play. The weight of the deception increased daily. The guests had arrived; each added to her guilt through their ready acceptance of her as Lord Adrian's wife. Indeed, Lord Adrian had gone out of his way to be the exemplary husband. Juliane could not decide what he was about.

It matters little, she thought; it will end the same

for me regardless of his design. But how to protect the children? She started as voices intruded into her ruminations.

"Lady Juliane—here you are," exclaimed Lady Stern. "Sir Percival and I wondered where you had gotten to."

"I felt the need to relax," Lady Juliane answered quietly.

"I can well understand that. This house has never seen so much excitement. My goodness, you are the best thing that could have happened. Is that not so, Sir Percival?"

"Yes, my lady, exactly so," beamed Sir Percival, twisting the lace on his sleeve, a habit Lady Juliane had patiently tried to ignore since being introduced to the foppish young man.

"You are both most kind," she replied.

Laughter edged into the room and they all turned to the door. Lord Adrian and one of the most beautiful women Lady Juliane had ever seen entered arm in arm.

"You have been negligent, Lord Adrian," said Lady Stern, tapping his arm with her fan, "for not having told us Lady Cecile was coming."

"But, I did not know it. Her presence is a delightful surprise provided by Mother." He sought Lady Juliane's eyes, but she looked away.

Noticing Lady Cecile's intimate manner and flirting glances at Lord Adrian, Juliane began having uncharacteristically unsavoury thoughts about the woman. She would swallow him, she thought distastefully. If she clung any closer, she might just as well be

169

a drape. A milk and toast miss if ever she saw one, she quipped silently to herself.

Juliane's thoughts continued in this caustic manner as she took in the perfect coiffure, the palest complexion, the slimmest figure with curves disgustingly well placed, and the tiniest of feet peeping from beneath a rose gown complete with furbelows and gewgaws. Repulsively feminine—the sort men had preferred throughout all of Lady Juliane's competently unfeminine life.

"Lady Juliane . . . I say, Lady Juliane?" repeated Sir Percival, with a nervous twist at his lace.

"Oh, yes, Sir Percival?"

"Lady Cecile," he coughed delicately into his lace, "was addressing you."

"Lady Cecile, I am sorry—what was it?" Lady Juliane asked in a sharper tone than she intended.

"I merely wished to offer you my most sincere congratulations," gushed Lady Cecile. "Why, you must realize you are the most fortunate of women—such a man as Lord Adrian," she hugged the arm she had continued clinging to. "To remove such a nonpareil from the marriage mart is a feat indeed. How did you manage it?"

Lady Juliane felt the hostility beneath Lady Cecile's soft tones and sensed Lord Adrian's discomfort. Failing to resist the urge, and dismissing her usual sense, she bubbled, "Why, I just cannot tell you." Taking Lord Adrian's free arm, she looked up adoringly and sighed. "He just swept me away—you know his ways. I could not resist his marvelous manners. Fortunately for me, he also had a penchant for honied water in crockery mugs," she cooed, while recall-

ing how she had halted his amourous advances at the
farm cottage.

The assembled company exchanged puzzled looks
as a slow blush crept above Lord Adrian's collar.
This was more nerve-wracking than any situation he
had ever found himself in. What had come over Juliane? He would have to have a word with Mother
also. He had no need of further complications.

"It is, perhaps, time we retired to our rooms,"
hinted Lady Stern. "Come, Lady Cecile, we must have
a nice coze before we sup."

Lady Cecile hesitated, then seeing that Lady Juliane was giving her attention to Sir Percival, she
agreed. "We must. It will be most delightful. You can
give me your opinion on my gown for tomorrow evening," she said, while smiling at Lord Adrian.

"I am sure you both will be breathtaking," Adrian
said, escorting the two ladies to the door.

"Then we must all be persuaded you will be
matchless," purred Lady Juliane, disengaging herself
from Sir Percy's arm. Instantly regretting her childish
cattishness, she brushed past those at the door and
did not even notice Count Cavilón as she hurried past
him to her room.

"You have been up to something, my friend,"
reproached the count, entering the salon Lady Juliane had just left. He made a slight bow as Lady Stern
and Lady Cecile excused themselves.

"Lady Juliane did not even notice my raiment," he
said with a sniff and a wave of his lace kerchief.

Sir Percival fidgeted with his lace. He was always
uncertain as to what action to pursue in the presence
of the count.

171

"Percy, you had better change for supper—your lace is wilting," snapped Lord Adrian.

"Oh, of course, Cousin Adrian. Till we sup, Count Cavilón." He bowed and retreated.

The count returned the bow perfunctorily and turned to face Adrian. "Why be so irritable with *le pauvre compagnon*? You are not yourself," he said, going to close the doors of the salon. "What has happened to those iron nerves of yours?"

"Enough of your foolishness, Louís. Did you have any success?"

"Whoever said the English were *sérieux*. You have the French *tempérament*." He smiled as Lord Adrian glowered at him, then becoming serious, lowered his voice. "I have had some *succès*. The four Frenchmen have evidently followed Lady Juliane and the children from France. They must have thought to find the information or whatever they seek on her maid. I believe they killed the maid because she could identify them and because they feared she would warn Lady Juliane. One, at least, is of the *aristocratie*. From the local gossip, fowl and other items have been disappearing since you arrived; therefore, they must be close by."

"Bah! That is nothing I do not already know."

"Ah, yes, but I received a letter delivered only this morning with information on Baron La Croix which I believe you will find *très intéressant*." Count Cavilón pulled the letter from an inner pocket and held it forward. "After you read this, you will be ready to lay plans."

*　　*　　*

Reaching her room, Lady Juliane slammed the door behind her. With the back of her hand she wiped away the tears that had come unbidden to her eyes. "Tears," she muttered angrily. "What kind of fustian behaviour is this? Find your backbone," she admonished herself. "Why let that bit of fluff bother you? She will wear out her eyelashes batting them at Lord Adrian. Why should I care if that is what he prefers—it'd serve him right to end up on her hook. She would make him squirm the rest of his life."

Lady Juliane found this thought quieting. Entering a short while later, Bess found her ladyship pensively staring into space.

"I am sorry I am late, your ladyship. We have all been pressed into extra duties, what with the ball being on the morrow. It will be the most glamourous thing I have ever seen. But come, my lady, you must dress or you will be late. Which gown will it be? The puce, or perhaps . . ."

"No," said Lady Juliane, rising. "The velvet mahogany."

Bess kept her smile hidden. News of Lady Cecile's arrival had spread rapidly among the household staff and it heartened Bess that Lady Juliane was finally taking interest in her appearance. This could only denote something interesting in the offing.

That evening Lady Juliane entered the salon quietly; she felt no need to draw undue attention to herself, for she felt the confidence of her appearance. Her glass's reflection had not told her she was beautiful, certainly not in the style of Lady Cecile, but it had been far from condemning. She had had Bess fetch Satter to powder her hair as soon as she had arranged it. The effect of this together with the mahogany gown, which not only suited her colouring but also flattered her figure, had evoked a very handsome reflection.

First to see her was Count Cavilón. He approached with an elegant swagger. "Lady Juliane, may I say you are *ravisante* this evening."

"You may say what you please, Count, as you are a close friend of my husband's," she said, smiling.

"Then I must add that my friend is the most fortunate of men to have found a treasure such as you," he bowed with a turn of his lace-covered hand.

"You are most flattering, my lord. May I say you too appear to be in the height of fashion this evening," she returned with a flutter of her fan.

"You are too kind, my lady. I fear I am a touch too elegant for the country," he protested.

"Of course not, my lord. You will provide much conversation for months to come—what more shall you wish for?" While speaking, her eyes had swept the room. She emphasized her conclusion by angrily snapping her fan shut.

Curious, Count Cavilón followed her gaze. It led to the far side of the room where Lord Adrian and Lady Cecile were engaged in a private chat.

Lady Tretain was appraised of Lady Juliane's presence by Holdt and ordered him to call the company to dinner. Her house guests were of a larger number than she preferred on this occasion. It would be twenty seated to dine tonight which would make the pre-ball supper number over thirty. With such numbers, anything could happen; she had heard of Lady Juliane and Lady Cecile's exchange.

Holdt intoned, "Dinner is served," and everyone rose.

"May I have the honour and pleasure of escorting you, Lady Juliane?" asked the count.

"You are most gracious," Lady Juliane said, smiling, as she saw the black look cross Lord Adrian's face. He had excused himself and was making his way to her.

His mother was quick to see this also. "So good of you to humour your mother, son," she said, laying a hand on his arm.

"Yes? Oh, of course, Mother. It has been some time since I have had the privilege of escorting you."

"Then let us not keep everyone waiting." She pulled at his sleeve, and he led the way.

Following directly behind, Count Cavilón thought the evening was going to be vastly more entertaining than he had dared hope. Lord Adrian had been reticent when it came to details concerning Lady Juliane, but the count was certain that each held the other in affection. Their behaviour made this apparent to everyone except the two concerned. That they had not confessed their love was clearly evident. He felt he could remedy this, perhaps not in as pleasant a mode as the pair would hope, but it would be far more diverting his way and would ensure a pleasant conclusion.

Throughout dinner Count Cavilón was witty and entertaining. Lady Juliane found herself losing her distaste for him, although she maintained her distrust. Seeing Lady Cecile seated beside Lord Adrian and amusing him charmingly, she abandoned herself to entertaining her dinner partners. From the black looks cast her way by both Lord Adrian and Lady

175

Tretain, she felt she was succeeding beyond her hopes.

When the men rejoined the women after taking their port, Count Cavilón once more sought out Lady Juliane's company and continued flattering her.

Lady Juliane had admitted to herself earlier that she found all this attention vastly enjoyable, even though she had no doubt it lacked serious intent. She was beginning to understand why some women went to any length to win it.

"I understand, my lady, that you are but recently come from Rouen. How did you find the atmosphere there?" the count asked, as he watched her eyes flick once again across to Lord Adrian and Lady Cecile.

"I fear things are seriously wrong there. You would not believe what occurred in Rouen," she said without thinking.

"Why do you not tell me, I feel I would believe anything you would tell me," cajoled the count smoothly. "I understand the La Croix family estates are near there; did it involve them?" he led her on.

"What do you know of them?" she asked, suspicion entering her voice.

"Only the barest of knowledge," laughed the count. He was certain she had almost yielded to the urge to trust him. He had yet to gain her confidence. "There are so many aristocratic families, you understand; one cannot know them all. There was some gossip about the baron the past few months—that is all," he shrugged negligently.

"Gossip?" She spread her fan with concentration. "Of course, all women are interested in gossip. You cannot mean to tantalize me with the hint of it without telling all," she said, raising her fan to her face.

"What could a minor French family mean to you?" he teased calculatingly.

"Nothing, of course. But come, what is it you heard?" Her laugh was a trifle nervous.

"If you insist—it seems the baron was becoming short of funds. He had an English wife who was angry with him—the remainder is very confusing. The story is being told in all different manners, but it concerns a small fortune in jewels. One never knows what to believe about gossip, does one?" he asked, watching her closely.

"No, of course not. It is probably all false," she said, fanning herself thoughtfully. "Come, let us join Lord Adrian." As she led the way, not allowing him to refuse, she tried to digest his words. Would it be the gems the abductors were after? Cora had mentioned nothing. In searching the house at Rouen she herself had found nothing. If only she had a clue to their pursuers' identities. Was the baron among them?

"A pleasant surprise to have you join us, my dear," said Lord Adrian. His grating tone brought her attention back to the present.

"But how could I refrain from your company an entire evening?" she asked in reply.

"Lady Cecile, would you join me?" asked Count Cavilón, bowing graciously.

"I would be delighted, my dear Count. It is a relief that some men present know how to amuse one," she said pointedly.

Watching the two walk away, Lady Juliane smiled deceptively. "Losing your charm, my lord?"

"No more than you are acquiring yours," he answered in like mien.

"My, my, feeling a touch raw this evening. Let me remind you, it is at your insistence that I remain. Are you now willing to renounce your plans for tomorrow evening?"

"No, my lady," he said firmly. "No one shall deny me the pleasure of presenting my wife."

"Whom is it you hate—your mother or myself?" she asked, feeling a tear prick behind her eyes.

"Now is no time to speak of it—later. Come," he took her arm, "let us make a foursome with Mother and Cousin Percy for a game of whist. I am sure you could find nothing more delightful." Juliane's answering look convinced him that their conversation was at an end.

18

Light flooded the room as Bess threw open the draperies and stripped back the bed hangings. "Oh, my lady, aren't you excited! The night will be here ere the wax is properly shined. I just knew you'd wish to be up early."

Lady Juliane turned over and covered her head with her pillow. Today was one day she would just as leave forget.

"No funning me now, Lady Juliane, best to be up. Lord Adrian sent word he will be visiting shortly," insisted Bess, certain this would rouse her Ladyship if nothing else could.

"Did he say when?" asked Lady Juliane, sitting up abruptly.

"No, my lady," answered Bess, bringing the cup of chocolate to her.

"Never mind that," Lady Juliane exclaimed, pushing the cup away. "Let me get dressed. Don't stand there gaping. What should I wear?" Jerking open the wardrobe, she began going through the gowns. "I think this blue day gown—why the frown? Oh, yes, my gown for this evening is blue—this won't do. Fiddle-faddle, you choose something while I do my hair," Lady Juliane said, her mind in such a dither she did not notice the connecting door open.

"Our ways have changed, haven't they, my dear?" He smiled, then became serious. "The value of the garments I have given you is increased tenfold by your pleasure in them."

Lady Juliane had swung around at the sound of Lord Adrian's voice. Viewing with increasing disfavour his impeccable appearance in buckskin breeches, wren-brown small clothes, and exquisitely cut buckskin coat, she asked, "Will you never learn to give some warning?"

"Bess, you may go. I will send for you when you are needed."

"No, Bess, stay here." After last night, Lady Juliane had no wish to be alone with him.

Bess's pained expression swung from Lord Adrian to Lady Juliane, then back to Lord Adrian. She bowed her head and stammered as she went out the door. "I'm . . . I'm sorry, my lady."

"You are detestable," Lady Juliane said calmly as the door closed.

"I am happy to learn your opinion is improving," Adrian said, seating himself. He waved his hand languidly. "That is charming in a countrified way, but I am convinced the negligee I had sent from London would suit your looks more favourably." He raised his quizzing glass.

Lady Juliane glanced down and realized she was still in her nightdress. Walking calmly to the bed where her wrapper lay, she tried to think of suitable revenge. The vile man had mentioned her attire only to embarrass her. She drew on the wrapper and turned smilingly to Lord Adrian. "What is it you wish to discuss, my lord?" she asked sweetly.

Lord Adrian cocked his head in turn, but offered no other sign of discernment. "I had not thought to find you in such a fair humour this morning. Shall I thank Louis for it?" His tone did not change but his look became cold, hard, and cynical.

"I do not know what you mean," she replied calmly, seating herself at her dressing table and picking up her comb.

Lord Adrian rose with the smooth motion of a panther and began pacing.

"What is it, my lord?" she asked, turning in her chair.

He stopped and stared as if trying to reach a decision concerning her. "I . . . I have ordered the children to remain in their rooms until tomorrow morning." His look cut her objection. "Fool! Can you not see this would be the perfect opportunity for the abductors? With all the additional help, stir, and fuss in getting the last details accomplished for this evening, they could easily enter the house undetected. I have taken additional steps to protect the children, but it is best if no one knows of it." He had become impassive once more. "I wish only to assure you that everything is being done for their safety. I ask only for your cooperation this evening."

"My cooperation, my lord?"

"I believe you know exactly what I mean." He approached her and lifted her head with his hand. "We shall present a very happy front to our guests this evening." His coldness flickered, then vanished to be replaced by an appeal. "I have arranged a very special surprise for you after the ball." His lips claimed Juliane's before she could object. She felt herself responding to the gentle question in the movement of his lips upon her own. Shaken, she could only stare when he drew back.

Taking her hand, Adrian withdrew the band she wore and slowly eased another ring in its place. He looked searchingly at her, his eyes pledging a love he had not voiced. "This is my token of our betrothal, Juliane," he said. Gently raising her hand, he kissed the newly placed ring and was gone.

Bess found her mistress still seated, staring blankly at the large diamond solitaire on her finger.

Lady Juliane spent the remainder of the day in a semihaze. She tended to the minor details Lady Tretain assigned her and visited with the children. They were unruly, affected by the fever pitch with which everyone bustled about. She had succeeded in calming them somewhat, when shouts outside drew them to the windows.

Near the front steps a rider was falling off a lathered horse. Holdt and a liveried servant rushed to help him.

"Who was that?" asked André, straining to see out the window.

"I have no idea—a messenger of some sort, I would guess by the state of his horse," Juliane answered. "I must go now. You help Alva amuse Leora. Perhaps she could play soldiers with you. You shall see me again before we dine; remember, you are not to leave these rooms," she cautioned.

As she went back into the hall, she wondered what to do. There was still some time left before she must dress and she did not feel like resting. A walk in the garden, she decided, would clear her mind. Glancing down at her hand, she touched the ring. It was real. Had Lord Adrian meant it as a sign of his love?

What to believe? The world had become strangely unhinged since she had left India. Everything seemed to swirl together, making it impossible to discern fact from fiction. Her head told her to question Lord Adrian's action. Her heart told her to depend on him; it told her she loved him.

Her natural honesty forced the conclusion upon her. Why else did she get so disconcerted when he was near; why else the jealousy of Lady Cecile; why else the thrill at his touch—at his kiss?

Hope. Hope bouyed her. Lord Adrian had appeared of serious mind despite his witticisms and off-hand manner. Precautions, he said, were being taken for the children. This had surprised her. She smiled to herself as she continued to wander aimlessly about the halls.

"There you are, Lady Juliane. Would you tell Holdt, if you see him, to be certain the extra grooms are liveried and wearing their gloves. Also check the flower arrangements in the ballroom. They were not completely finished with them when I left." Lady Tretain sighed tiredly. "I must rest if I am to make it through this night."

Impulsively, she hugged a startled Lady Juliane. "I know I am not the easiest of women to abide, but Adrian has eased my fears concerning you by telling me of your plans for after the ball. It is an odd choice in time, but then he is so like his father, sensible until he takes a notion. You have done him so much good.

"I must go to my bed; see to it that you get some rest also. Must be in fine fettle, you know."

Lady Juliane's eyes followed Lady Tretain's stately walk down the hall, baffled. What had Lady Tretain meant by her mind being eased? Best not to try and understand this family, she reasoned. Be thankful when they show some sense. Try as she might, she could not stifle the "but why" echoing in her mind.

A while later, Lady Juliane lay back on her bed, trying to rest. She had done all that had been bidden of her, even finding time for another visit to the children before yielding to Bess and permitting her to close the draperies and have her lie down.

Juliane was far too keyed up to sleep. All day she had been constantly fingering the ring Lord Adrian had given her. She tried to deduce his plan, his surprise, but her thoughts led to the remembrance of his tender glances, the thrill of his touch. Reason told her he could not have told his mother what it was if it were anything less than honourable. Could it be? His actions and looks bespoke affection, perhaps love for her, but she longed for the assurance of words. Love had been a stranger long in coming, and she was afraid to trust her judgment alone. Her thoughts whirled in confusion . . .

"Time to be up and about, my lady," said Bess.

"They will dine earlier than usual this night and we mustn't keep them waiting."

Lady Juliane opened her eyes. Had she truly fallen asleep? The shadowed sky was her answer. "Goodness, Bess, why did you allow me to sleep so late?"

"Never fear, my lady, your hip bath is ready for you. Let me unfasten you now. Go on in, I'll lay out your things. Call as soon as you're ready for the towel. I have it warming."

Lady Juliane untied her wrapper as she walked across the room. She had found the small corner room equipped as a lavatory the most decided luxury in the house. Removing her wrapper, she stuck a hand tentatively in the water—perfect. She eased herself in, relaxing in the warmth.

"Now, my lady," Bess bustled in, carrying the large towel that had been warmed before the fire. "We mustn't dawdle. I have everything laid out and Satter will be here shortly. Do you think after the ball I might try my hand at powdering your hair? I've been practicing and think I could do it."

Letting Bess chatter on, Lady Juliane dressed. The sound of her voice was soothing, like the babble of a spring.

"Ah, la, my lady, the gown must be the latest from London. I have never seen anything like it."

"Yes, I feel positively naked with only two petticoats but I dare not wear my pannier; anything more than the hip pads will ruin its lines," Juliane reasoned, more to herself than to Bess. Lady Juliane had seen such gowns in Lady Tretain's latest fashion magazines but had never thought to wear one herself.

"Come, come," fluttered Satter, as she entered all in

a pother. "We must hurry this, I still have so much to do for Lady Tretain and you know, no one can please her as I do."

Satter held out the floor-length frock coat which was meant to protect the wearer's undergarments. Managing Lady Juliane expertly into it, she seated her and went deftly to work. Miffed because she had not been asked to comb her ladyship's hair, she sniffed at the lack of height and breadth to the style. When she had completed the dusting, the last auburn tress whitened, Satter begrudgingly allowed the effect was most becoming. Classic in detail, it set off Lady Juliane's facial lines and the soft curls lessened the severity into courtly elegance.

Satisfied, Satter removed the frock coat and whisked out of the room without waiting for a dismissal or a thank you.

"Oh, my lady," breathed Bess. "You are . . ."

"Let us refrain from judgment until we have the complete effect. Do you think it is time for the gown?"

"Yes, my lady. Best to be a step ahead instead of three behind. Let me fetch Nell, she's been helping Alva. We don't want to chance crushing it."

While she waited, Lady Juliane walked to the wardrobe. The gown had been hung on a pole across the open doors since early afternoon. Hesitantly, she reached out. The gown did not disappear at her touch, she was not dreaming.

"I hope you won't mind my bringing Alva, my lady?"

"Should you have left the children, Alva?"

"Nell is watching them, and Bess said this won't be takin' long. I so wished to help," pleaded Alva.

"All right, but let us hurry. We must not take chances with their safety. Will you watch them closely this evening? There will be many strangers about," counseled Lady Juliane.

"Aye, m'lady. What do I do, Bess?"

"You have to help guide the skirts. Step up into that chair, my lady."

"In the chair?"

"It's the only way I know of to get you into it without crushing it," assured Bess.

This maneuver done, not without many girlish giggles on the part of all, Bess eased the sleeves up, one at a time.

"Now for the fastening. Alva, I think that's all we need you for. You can go back to the children."

"Away with that frown," said Juliane. "I will visit the nursery before we go down. Tell the children I will be there soon and—thank you," said Juliane, smiling.

Bess began hooking the buttons—they ran from neck to mid-hip. After working down to mid-back and then up from the bottom she said, "My lady, I think we will have to tighten your stays a bit." She was surprised at the demure acquiescence, for it had taken quite a bit to convince Lady Juliane even to try the half-boned corset.

Tightening completed, the last dozen buttons were tugged through their loops. Bess straightened and flounced the skirt, then stepped back to appraise the effect. She turned Lady Juliane to the glass. "Look, my lady."

The reflection amazed Lady Juliane. The gown, of finest sky-blue silk, overlayed with the sheerest of silver silks, was breathtaking. Fashionable off-shoulder, tiny rosettes of matching colour formed shoulder straps and ran down either side of the center front insert to the floor. The delicately gathered skirt flowed from the waist at side and back. Sequins had been worked in small floral patterns on the bottom third of the skirt and also over the full, half-sleeves.

"My lady, I found these in the box that the dress was in. What would they be for?" asked Bess, holding single blue and silver rosettes in her hand.

"I . . . Why, would they not enhance my hair? The pins, let us try this. Yes, I do believe—what do you think?" she asked, seeking assurance.

"Just the right touch, my lady. You are so lovely," sighed Bess.

Lady Juliane turned slowly in front of the glass. She felt lovely.

"I shall see the children before Lord Adrian is ready."

"No, my lady. We shall see the children together," Lord Adrian said, entering through the connecting door. To Mallatt, who was following him carrying a small wooden chest, he said, his voice full of pride, "Did I not tell you?" He waved a hand toward Lady Juliane.

"Yes, my lord," answered Mallatt. He bowed deeply to Juliane. "You are most lovely, my lady."

"Thank you, Mallatt," she answered, shyness entering her voice.

"I will take that, Mallatt, you may go. Bess, you may leave also."

Mallatt winked knowingly at Bess and crossed the room, ushering her out. He knew of the betrothal ring and of the plans for after the ball and was determined that no one disturb the pair this time.

Lady Juliane grew increasingly nervous under Lord Adrian's scrutiny. "You are looking most handsome this evening, my lord," she managed to say.

Running an appraising eye over his evening dress, she took in the formfitting breeches and coat, which were of a sky-blue silk matching her gown. The small clothes were of silver silk; gracing his immaculate white shirt lace, a lighter blue cravat matched his stockings. Silver shoes with sparkling silver buckles completed his ensemble. A modest periwig was the crowning touch. She knew they would be a striking pair.

"You lack but one thing. As Lady of the House of Tretain, you must wear these." Lord Adrian opened the wooden chest and withdrew a simple tiara fashioned in diamonds which he carefully settled in her hair. Next, he handed her droplet earrings and, as she fastened them on, he said, "I had this piece cleaned especially for you. It arrived along with something else of import this afternoon. I hope you approve." Slowly he raised a stunning diamond necklace.

As he secured it about her neck, she watched in the glass. Fingering it, she realized it was a simple rendering of the Tretain crest.

Raising her eyes, she became captivated by his as he stared at their reflection.

"Absolutely exquisite," he breathed as he slowly turned her to face him. Pride and tender passion covered his features. Slowly he embraced Juliane, drawing her very close. She did not resist his lips as they claimed her own, but answered their gentle movement with a surge of feeling that startled her. Adrian responded hungrily and some time passed before he eased his hold and looked pensively at her.

Juliane's mind searched for words, her heart pounding tumultuously. "My lord," she began shakily.

"Adrian," he corrected with a slow smile.

"My lord . . . Adrian . . . we shall be late. I . . . I promised the children . . ." She was stayed by his look.

The softness had left his expression, a question replacing it. He smiled tersely and made a leg. "Your wish is my command, for this night at least." A twinkle lit his eyes.

"*I*, dare to command *you*, my lord? Who could judge me guilty of that?" she asked, attempting to equal his bantering tease.

Both felt their relationship had been altered, deepened, but a further probing would have to wait until after the ball.

Becoming conscious that they both had suddenly become very prim, the pair exchanged a bow and curtsy with mock seriousness, then broke into laughter.

Warmth and security enveloped Juliane as she took Adrian's proffered hand and walked slowly to the nursery.

19

Morton opened the door to the nursery for them as they approached. Lord Adrian remained at his side for a few moments, checking over instructions, while Lady Juliane entered.

Alva hastily grabbed both Leora and André's hands to prevent them from running to Lady Juliane and mussing her gown.

Lord Adrian entered as Juliane finished a slow pirouette before them. André, his eyes shining, clapped enthusiastically. Less interested, Leora was drawn by the flash of the sequins as the skirt swirled, the light of the setting sun causing them to glitter.

"You are most beautiful," said André softly. Tears suddenly sprung to his eyes. "I cannot but think of . . ." Swallowing hard, he ran and threw himself upon his bed, breaking into sobs.

Leora was baffled by her sibling's action. *"Ma mère, ma mère,"* she cooed.

Lady Juliane walked to her and held her hand for a moment. "Alva, take Leora into the other room for a moment." Letting go of Leora's hand, she went to André and, sitting on the bedside near him, placed a hand comfortingly on his back, rubbing it slowly.

"I am sorry," he gulped out between sobs.

"Do not be, André," Juliane answered softly. "I understand. We will talk about it on the morrow. Now, dry your tears. You do not wish to spot my gown," she teased gently, trying to draw him out. She felt an overwhelming sadness. Her appearance in ball dress could not have failed to evoke memories of a mother who loved parties far better than anything else.

I should have thought of it, she mused to herself, unhappy to have caused sadness on what looked to be a joyful night.

"André, your *tante* Juliane will believe herself unfit for the ball if you continue your crying," added Lord Adrian, taking one of Juliane's hands in his. "Do you not think she is lovely?"

Juliane looked up at Adrian. His eyes told her that he knew most of the story—that he too wished to ease the boy's melancholy thoughts.

Sitting up and wiping his tears away, André flashed a weak smile.

"That is much better," smiled Lady Juliane in return. "We must go now. Obey Alva and let no one enter your rooms."

"Can I not see you dance?" he asked.

"Not this evening, son," answered Lord Adrian. "But you may watch our very next ball—all night if you wish."

"Oh, *merci.*" Thinking on it a moment, he frowned. "That will be so long from now."

"No," laughed Lord Adrian, tousling André's curls. "It will be but six weeks hence, soon after we open our house in London. I will tell you more tomorrow," he said, not only to André, but also in answer to Lady Juliane's questioning look.

"Alva," he called, "make certain the doors are secured."

"Aye, m'lord," she answered, returning to the room.

"Let us go, Juliane. I cannot wait to see Louís's expression."

"He cannot help but appreciate our appearance, although he may not be pleased with your looks," she said, a sparkle showing.

"Why is that?"

"Your attire cannot but put his to shame this evening, my lord."

Lord Adrian halted at the top of the stairs. "You will never succeed with flattery. Besides, I thought we had reached an understanding." Placing a kiss lightly upon her lips, he said sternly, "I will do this every time you fail to call me by name this evening."

Blushing, Lady Juliane blurted, "You would not dare."

"We shall see. Your hand, my dear," he said, raising his. "We must make a suitably formal entrance."

Holdt watched the pair glide gracefully down the stairs. Although he succeeded in tempering a smile at his pleasure in them, he failed to hide his pride. As the two continued toward him, he stepped through the double doors into the drawing room and announced sonorously: "Lord Adrian, Earl of Tretain and Lady Juliane, Countess of Tretain."

Juliane felt a thrill sweep through her at his words. If only it could be. She looked at Adrian and was bouyed by the love she saw in his eyes.

Silence was broken only by their footsteps as Holdt's announcement ended. Everyone was staring. Lord Adrian led Lady Juliane to his mother. She curtised low as Lord Adrian made a leg.

"My children, you are an assured success." She took Juliane's hand. "Tomorrow and all the days after you shall reign rightfully as Lady Tretain. No," she stopped Juliane from speaking, "as much as I dislike the title, I am most pleased to be the dowager countess." Lady Juliane thought she saw a tear in Lady Tretain's eye, but the older woman snapped her fan open and turned.

"Count Cavilón, you will have the honour of escorting me this evening," she ordered, pointing at him with her fan.

"I am most pleased to be so distinguished," he answered. "Lady Juliane, may I say you are *très belle* this evening?" he added.

"Only when I am present," interposed Lord Adrian lightly.

The count smiled and nodded; he had noticed the pair's new rapport, their beaming faces and loving gazes.

"Holdt, what are you waiting for? Announce dinner. I do not wish to be rushed," said Lady Tretain, placing her hand on Cavilón's arm. "We will follow you, my son," she added, smiling her approval.

"As you wish, Mother. Juliane."

The dinner went well. Sitting beside Lord Adrian, Lady Juliane found it a much more pleasant experience than the previous evening.

Lord Adrian pointed out various neighbours who had been invited, adding pithy remarks to each name. Lady Juliane's enjoyment and confidence increased as the meal progressed and she acknowledged the highly complimentary looks she was receiving.

Then, much later, in looking from Lord Adrian to the Marquess of Bout, who was seated on her other side, Lady Juliane caught sight of Holdt, whispering in Lady Tretain's ear.

Nodding at his words, Lady Tretain signaled to Lady Juliane that it was time to rise. Lord Adrian had also seen Holdt and, after exchanging mutual "now it begins" looks, he stood. Immediately the remainder of the company rose. Lady Tretain, Lord Adrian, and Lady Juliane walked slowly to their places in the receiving line just outside the ballroom.

"I have long dreamed of this day, my son—as you well know. You have made me very proud and happy," Lady Tretain said as the first guests reached them.

"Do not be nervous, my dear," she added to Lady Juliane. "You could not be more lovely."

"You see, I am not alone in my views. Now you must believe me," smiled Lord Adrian, giving her hand a reassuring squeeze. "This will be over soon. Curiosity will prevent anyone being tardy in arriving. That is the custom in London, but not here."

Nothing in Lady Juliane's previous experiences had prepared her for her position in the receiving line. Accustomed to assuming an unobtrusive position at the functions she had hosted for her brother, she was almost overwhelmed by the attention now shown her. Her hand felt as if it would never recover from the clutches and crushes it received. Never had it been subjected to so many gallant kisses or her person to so many compliments. Finding it all tremendously uplifting, she completely forgot her worries, and faced the prospect of the actual ball with more enthusiasm.

Lady Tretain motioned it was time to enter the ballroom. Placing a kiss lightly on her gloved hand, Lord Adrian laughed quietly. "Courage, Juliane. The inspection we are about to receive will be most critical. They will judge us and therefore feel free to dismiss us from their minds."

Lady Juliane felt a slight tremour. She had never been the focus of attention in such a crush.

Noticing this, Lord Adrian whispered as they paused, waiting for the orchestra to strike their entrance theme, "Courage. Envision all the periwigs and perukes of our elegant guests in danger of toppling off."

This drew the desired smile as the orchestra sounded the first chord. Looking the length of the ballroom as they entered, Lady Juliane was stayed from faltering by Lord Adrian's suggestion and the reassurance of his firm hold upon her hand. Viewing the richly clad assembly as he had advised certainly made them less imposing.

The required opening dance was mercifully brief. Leading the next set, they were joined by their guests, and soon the floor was filled by dancing, laughing couples.

At the end of the set, a swarm of men surrounded Lady Juliane, demanding a place on her dance program. Realizing she had received none, she looked to Lord Adrian, and found him watching with amused certainty.

"You must need apply to my lord, I fear," she found herself saying.

"Tretain, this is unheard of," complained one.

"Outrageous," added another.

"Her ladyship's card is filled," he answered carelessly, and would not be swayed. His eyes were for Juliane alone.

Later that evening, as Lord Adrian led her out for the sixth quadrille, Juliane whispered, "My . . . Adrian, they will surely think this odd. You cannot mean to dance all evening only with me—it is . . . it will be regarded as insulting."

"I will perform my duties as host, never fear. As I was never known to be constantly on the floor, they will think me totally smitten with you, and forgive me. Do you not realize they will find pleasure in seeing me totally blinded by love?"

The first he said lightly. The second caused a thrill to run through her. Was she correct in the depth of feeling she read in his features?

Count Cavilón appeared to lead Lady Juliane from the floor while Lord Adrian chatted with his guests. Signaling for a footman to bring refreshments, the count sat down next to her. The ballroom did not seem quite as crowded as it had appeared several hours earlier in the evening.

Taking the champagne, he handed a goblet to Lady Juliane and began sipping at his own.

"This must be my last," she laughed. "I feel it is going to my head."

"You are happy then?" the count asked in sudden seriousness.

"Of course. Is that not an odd question?"

"What has Louis been up to? Bringing such a frown to your lips is unforgivable on this night," interrupted Lord Adrian. "It is the last dance, my dear, and I claim it," he added.

Juliane allowed him to lead her out, giving Count Cavilón an uneasy glance. The dance did nothing to alleviate her sudden apprehension as the steps allowed little conversation. With every chance she looked to Count Cavilón. He was watching her closely —speculatively, she thought.

Everything had been so perfect up to that unexpected question—that "are you happy?" But had not André's tears put the first pall on the night? The situation was far from perfect. She must be careful not to lose herself in a dream world.

Nothing was guaranteed for the children, least of all their safety. She herself was foolishly in love with this cool, stark man she knew little about and who passed her off as his wife as if it were a usual experience. Where had her reason gone?

As the music faded slowly away, she realized that someone was calling her name.

"Juliane. Juliane? Is something wrong?" Lord Adrian asked.

She turned and looked at him—stepping back, tugging her hand from his.

"What is it?" he asked urgently.

"Oh, children. There you are." Lady Tretain's

voice infringed upon them. Glancing from one to the other, she asked "Why, has something occurred? What is upsetting you, Juliane?"

"Nothing," she answered hollowly.

"You must bid farewell to your guests," Lady Tretain continued, glancing slowly from one to the other.

"Come, Juliane." Lord Adrian held out his hand. Ignoring it, she walked through the crowd to the doors.

It seemed an eternity for the guests to exclaim upon the success of the ball and their enjoyment at meeting her, and finally take their leave. All the while she smiled and murmured the expected pleasantries, while her mind worked furiously. Had she been led into a false aura of safety? Was she deceiving herself in trusting Adrian? The present situation could not go on indefinitely. The more she thought, the stronger became her conviction that it must end—and tonight.

Lady Juliane would have been amazed to learn that Lord Adrian's thoughts and plans coincided with hers. He had some days earlier reached the same conclusion—circumstances could not be tolerated as they were. His feelings were far too involved. He had reached what he considered a feasible solution, but his indomitable male ego kept him from appraising Juliane of his decision.

Suddenly the hall was empty—they were alone. Whatever straightening and cleaning was required would be seen to after first light by order of Lady Tretain, who appreciated her servants and treated them well. At three in the morning servants and houseguests alike sought their beds willingly.

Lady Juliane looked about. It seemed everyone had magically disappeared; there was no sign of Lady Tretain, who had hovered near all evening. Only Lord Adrian remained and he had a most peculiar look. If she could think it possible, she would have supposed the look to be one of trepidation? Occupied with her own problems as she was, she did naught but note it.

"I . . ." Lord Adrian hesitated. A barrier was once more between them. "I suppose you are exhausted?"

"I have not really had time to think what I am," Juliane answered truthfully.

"Would you be so obliging as to walk with me? There is something I wish to show you and, more importantly, some news I must impart." Taking her arm, he guided her slowly through the house. Reaching the end of the used portion, he stopped and searched Lady Juliane's face.

"There is little you do not seem to know already, my lord."

Before she realized her error, he was kissing her, holding her tightly, crushing her to his lean, hard body as his lips demanded satisfaction. "My lord," she breathed questioningly when he loosened his hold. This caused him to claim her lips once more and Juliane's heart overrode her mind once more as she answered his passion with her own.

Reluctantly, Lord Adrian drew back from her. "My decision was correct," he stated breathlessly to himself. To Juliane he added, "You see, my dear, I always keep my word. Come, they are awaiting us."

Still swirling in the rapture of his embrace, she could make no sense of his words. "Who is waiting?"

"You shall see. This part of the house is not used these days. At the end of this corridor is what once was the family chapel, although I doubt it has been used even during my father's time. I have had a surprise prepared which I hope will please you." He smiled, entreating her approval.

Lady Juliane stopped him. "Adrian . . . what is it you have in mind?" she asked, suddenly wary.

"Will you not be surprised?" he answered.

"I feel it best not to be." She refused to move. "Now tell me."

Adrian shifted his weight nervously as she stood waiting. "It is the most sensible solution, you know," he managed to stumble out, fear of rejection hobbling his usual glibness.

"Sensible solution—to what?" she asked faintly.

"You could not escape from this unscathed—not unless there was no need to escape . . ." his look beseeched her understanding.

"This loss of words is most inopportune. Perhaps on the morrow you will feel more talkative." She turned but he locked her hand in his.

"You cannot go. This must be done. You cannot object—it is your honour that will be maintained. The House of Tretain is old and highly thought of." He paused to gaze deeply into her eyes. "And you do not find me totally repulsive."

Understanding his words and yet not, Juliane sought only to escape. Joy would have been boundless had he given the one reason she sought, but he had not. In truth, it seemed expediency was what he wished.

"I will be willing to adopt the children if it is possible," he urged her. "They will never want for anything."

She looked searchingly at him but his face had become impassive, chilling her. Her fingers were growing numb in the clench of his hands.

"Why the tears, Juliane?" he asked more softly. "This is not my sensible one." He gently wiped them away. "You are no young miss. There is no way out of this and it is more my fault than yours. Come, follow my lead. The special license arrived this afternoon." Taking one of her hands, he led her to the doors at the far end and knocked.

There was a pause. Then the doors slowly opened to reveal a small chapel dimly lit with candles. Large bouquets of white hothouse flowers of all kinds filled the side aisles and altar. A cleric in flowing robes, holding an open prayer book, awaited them.

Someone put a large bouquet of white roses mixed with baby's breath in Lady Juliane's hands. She stared in disbelief.

Forms to the side began taking shape as they walked down the short aisle. Lady Tretain, Sir Percival, and Count Cavilón were all there.

Juliane heard words spoken solemnly, questions asked. The answers she spoke seemed to come from far away, not from her own lips at all. A numbing coldness pervaded her. Then it was over and they were surrounded, being congratulated, kissed.

"So beautiful, my son," said Lady Tretain. "So happy." She dabbed at her eyes.

"Best wishes to you both," offered Count Cavilón.

Sir Percival stood silently by, making a shambles of what remained of his lace.

As the count and Sir Percy left the chapel, Lady Tretain, who had become silent, detained Lady Juliane. "You must forgive me, Juliane, for . . . for all my doubts concerning you. Adrian has told me how hurriedly you had to be married—the loss of your sister. Your niece and nephew shall always be treated as my own.

"When he said you both wished for a simple renewal of your vows in our own family chapel—well, I was so relieved. You do forgive me?" She spoke with such earnestness that Juliane laid a hand on her arm in reassurance.

"You are not the one needing forgiveness."

Lady Tretain shook her head. Taking Adrian's and Juliane's hands, she placed them together. "A long life and many blessings—the best of which is sharing." She blinked back tears of remembrance. "Good night, my dears."

Once more they stood alone. Neither spoke. Finally Lord Adrian coughed. "We cannot spend the night here."

Lady Juliane flung him a look which spoke "why not?"

"You must be very tired. Let us go to our rooms," he urged.

The long walk from the chapel seemed magically and frighteningly brief. Before she could forestall it, they were in the corridor outside their rooms. Seeing the guards at the children's door, she stalled. "We must check on the children."

Lord Adrian quickly agreed, in truth not feeling as dauntless as he pretended to be.

Quietly they entered. Lady Juliane tiptoed to the large cradle, Lord Adrian walked softly to the bed. Each slowly picked up the coverlets before them, so as not to awaken the child beneath.

Startled look flew to startled look as the coverlets were dropped—only pillows were beneath them—the children were gone.

20

Filled with disbelief, Lady Juliane tore the covers from the cradle, searching futilely. "Alva!" she called, running to the trundle bed in the corner. "Alva!" Grabbing the blankets she pulled viciously, only to see a line of pillows. "My God," she said blankly.

Lord Adrian, at last mobilized, called the guards in and questioned them closely.

Lady Juliane sank down on the trundle bed, clutching one of the pillows to herself as she listened to Adrian's questions. Self-reproach filled her; self-condemnation for all her actions, from the moment she had set foot inside the house at Rouen to the present, rose within her.

Lord Adrian led her to her room and seated her upon her bed. "I will call Bess," he said gently. "This has been too great a shock. At first light we shall be after them."

Angry, hurt, and desperately afraid for the children, Juliane vented her feelings on Lord Adrian. "You promised," she said, breaking the silence that had begun to alarm Adrian. "You promised them safety—you said extra precautions were being taken. What kind of man are you? What have you done to them?" she challenged through flowing tears. "I thought you loved me. I married you. What else can you want?"

"You are beside yourself, Juliane," he answered coldly. "I have nothing to gain from their disappearance."

"Then why did you try to have André abducted that day from the garden and why did you stop us from leaving?"

"If you will recall, we drove off four men that day," he said sadly. "I will order something sent up to soothe you. There is much for me to see to."

"Where are you going?" she asked, alarmed.

"Does it matter what I answer?" he asked tiredly. "You will believe only what you wish." With two long strides, he was gone from the room.

In a few moments Bess entered, wringing her hands. "Oh, my lady, what a terrible thing! Who could be so low?"

Lady Juliane sat on the bed, holding her head, trying to think.

"What is wrong with me?" Bess reprimanded herself. "I must get you tucked in. Here, will you rise, my lady, so I can unhook you—there now, you'll be feeling better soon . . ." On and on she rattled. Lady Juliane responded as though drugged.

Finally coming to a fuller consciousness, she found

herself placed neatly in bed. Bess was admonishing her to drink from a cup she placed in her hands.

Disliking the taste, she pushed it away.

"No" came a hard tone. "You are to drink it all. I will not leave until you do so."

Juliane looked up. The changeling man who had kissed her lovingly and wed her just an hour past, stood at the foot of her bed. His eyes were cold and hard and his face was drawn with fatigue. She felt that somehow she could ease his despair. Aching to do so but not knowing how, she raised the cup and gulped down the offending liquid. Lowering it, she saw that he was gone.

Bess settled Juliane back onto the pillows and she fell into a deep sleep.

Striding the halls to Count Cavilón's room, Lord Adrian strove to remove the white, accusing face from his thoughts. To know Lady Juliane did not trust him had cut him to the core. But his personal grief must be submerged until the children were found. Only with their return could she be made to realize her error. He cursed his own foolishness. His attempts at cat and mouse had failed miserably—now to salvage what he could.

Throwing the door open, he stalked to the bed and shook the count ruthlessly.

"What is the meaning of this abomination?" spluttered Cavilón, rising. "Why Tretain," he was taken aback. "What are you doing here?"

"The children have been taken."

"*Impossible!* But when?"

"Get dressed—I will explain the little I know. We

have much to learn, I fear. We must call in those we have had searching and see what has been learned. What a fool I was!"

"But what of the precautions . . ."

"Useless," Tretain cut him short. "Not only the children, but their nurse is missing as well. The guards know nothing."

"*C'est impossible.* Something had to be noticed. Now, I am ready—there is much to do before dawn gives us light. Never fear, *mon ami.* We will find them."

After a brief conference they went their separate ways. Both were grim when they met over the breakfast table a few hours later.

"What would you think, Louis? Will they expect us to launch a search? Why not give them something to think on? If nothing happens today, they cannot help but be curious. I do not think they really want the children."

"I agree. If we maintain a facade of ease, they may show their hand."

"Let us continue to search with the men we have been using. They may stumble across something. I will inform the guards. Otherwise, we will keep the news of the abduction quiet. Everyone and everything must appear normal."

Consciousness slowly returned to Lady Juliane. Her eyes blinked in the dim light of the draped bed. The confusion and uncertainty of the night were gone.

Stripping back the drapery, she jumped from the bed. First she must learn what Adrian had done; then she must decide upon a course of action.

Peeking into the hall, she saw the guards still standing at the children's door. Clicking the door shut, she asked herself why they would be there—to what purpose? Was last night a nightmare? Glancing down at her left hand, she dismissed that idea. The wedding band was proof enough of the night's events.

Not able to face Bess's chatter, she did not call for her maid but dressed alone as quickly as she could. Her first step would be to try and find some clue as to how the children had been taken. The first place to examine would be their rooms.

"Why are you still here?" she asked the guards, pausing at the nursery door.

"Lord Tretain's orders" was the only reply.

The room remained as she remembered it, the beds apart, but nothing else disturbed. Searching, she found only a few sets of clothing gone and oddly enough several of André's toy soldiers were missing from the shelf. Perhaps Alva had thought to take them so he could have something familiar with him, she reasoned. It was strange they had taken Alva with them, but a hopeful sign as well. They could not mean to harm the children if they took pains to provide someone to help care for them.

Having learned all she could from the rooms, she went in search of Lord Adrian. With some surprise, she found him in the small salon, visiting casually with Count Cavilón.

"My lord . . . Adrian," she hastily corrected herself, "I would have thought . . ."

"What would you have thought, my dear?"

"What is being done to find the children?" she demanded. "Why are you here?"

"You believe me responsible for their disappearance; if that is true, it would be rather silly for me to be rushing about supposedly trying to find them," he answered sarcastically.

Taken aback by this totally unexpected reply, Lady Juliane gasped. She stared in wonder, then fled the room, running until she was safely in her room. Slamming the door shut, she leaned against it, her heart torn by his words and look.

Why, he had all but confirmed her worst fears, and in front of Cavilón as well. There was nothing left but for her to take matters into her own hands, regardless of the consequences to herself.

Bess entered and was told to fetch the smallest valise she could find. Returning, she handed it to Lady Juliane who tossed it onto the bed. Helping her ladyship into the starkest riding habit she could find, Bess found herself dismissed. The valise was then stuffed with items deemed necessary. Strapping it shut, Lady Juliane took a long, slow look about her and sighed heavily. If only circumstances could have been different.

Going to her jewelry case, she slipped off the two rings Lord Adrian had given her and replaced them with her mother's wedding band.

Lady Juliane held Adrian's rings tightly for a long moment. Bidding farewell to all the hopes she had cherished, both knowingly and unknowingly, she walked firmly through the connecting passageway into Adrian's room. It did not take long to locate the tray in which his cufflinks and cravat pins were placed. She could trust Mallatt to give the rings to him if he happened to find them first. Two tears dropped unbidden onto the tray as she placed the rings there. Biting her lip, she quickly searched the bureau beneath and found what she needed.

Racing back to her room, she quickly reopened the valise and put the pistol within. Then, grabbing her cloak and taking up the valise, she hurried through the back corridors to the stables.

Although surprised to see Lady Juliane at such an early hour, cloak and valise in hand, the grooms dared not refuse her authoritarian orders. Quickly, they readied the spirited mare she selected.

"The mare is ready, your ladyship, but please, wait only a moment until I am ready. You are not familiar with our countryside and should not be out alone," pleaded the groom, certain the master's wrath would fall on him if he allowed Lady Juliane to go out unescorted a second time.

"I will not go far. I have need of air. Give me a leg up," she ordered, ignoring his protest. "Let go of her head." Settled in the saddle, she urged the mare out at a spanking pace. No one could stop her now.

Only when she reined the mare to a halt on a knoll past the woods did she realize how foolish she had been. She wanted to rush back to the house. But with Adrian's pistol she was safe enough—she knew how to use one, and she knew the lay of the land better than anyone supposed. In her idle hours the library had yielded many interesting facts about the Tretain estate.

Studying a map she had copied, she chose a direction. The map was old, but precisely detailed. Some of the huts and farms shown on it were certain to be

211

abandoned by now. It was her intent to search them, for she felt one of them had to contain the children.

By noon Juliane had covered but a tiny portion of the countryside and all the huts she had found had been occupied. She grimaced—the hostility and suspicion of the inhabitants was the last thing she had expected. On reflection, she should have known better. A lady of Quality did not galavant over the rural countryside asking questions and traveling unattended without raising suspicions.

As dusk began to fall, Juliane shuddered. Her cloak warded off this early chill but what of the night? The mare also was showing signs of displeasure, wanting its ration of grain and warm stall.

Veering from a clump of trees that had taken on an eerie form, her mount stumbled. Lady Juliane managed to keep her seat but the valise tumbled to the ground.

"Drat!" she expostulated. To retrieve it meant dismounting, no problem in itself, but remounting was another matter. Deciding that a solution would present itself, she slipped to the ground. The valise recovered, she tied it securely to the saddle and led the mare on.

Darkness swooped down as dusk abandoned her and she was hard put to keep her courage up. The previously silent landscape came suddenly alive with sounds of eerie and menacing import. Croaks, hoots, tweaks all took on spectral airs. Even the snapping of twigs beneath her feet and the thump of the mare's hooves were startling.

Moving forward, listening to every sound, time dragged on. Lady Juliane had no concept of how long she had been walking when a large, dark shape loomed before her. Stopping, she studied it, trying to determine exactly what it was. With caution, she approached. It appeared to be a hut of sorts—perhaps an old barn or stable. Shelter for the night at least, she thought. If only it was uninhabited.

Certain that her thudding heart could be heard by anyone and anything, she slowly approached the hut. Stopping short at what she thought were footsteps, she listened intently. Hearing nothing further, she assured herself all was well.

A few more steps brought her to the door. She knocked timidly, then more firmly. The door creaked slowly open.

"Is anyone here?" Juliane asked shakily.

By magic, a light appeared and a voice spoke. *"Oui, madame.* How kind of you to join us."

Turning to flee, she fell into the arms of a second man who had appeared behind her. In a wild glance she saw that a third man had hold of the mare.

"With your presence, Lady Perrill, our group is complete," said a refined, masculine voice. "Will you not step inside?"

21

"Were you not a bit *rigoureux* on her, Adrian? She has not had an easy time of it." Count Cavilón spoke softly to his friend.

"And what have I had? Damnation." Rising, he strode to the fire. "I did not mean that," he said slowly to no one. "Something seems to come over me when I am near her."

"Love is often like that, *mon ami,*" answered the count quietly. "You are fortunate to have found someone who loves you as you love her. Do not throw your love away on a misunderstanding."

Lord Adrian pivoted to face him, his face as black as the count had ever seen it. "You do not understand."

"I comprehend more than you can know. I know that we alone suffer when we let pride and obstinacy stop us from doing what we really want to do, or from saying what we should." He paused. "Or from

unsaying that which never should have been said."
Cavilón laid a hand on Adrian's back. "I have been where you are now," he said sadly, "and I failed. By all I know true, Juliane loves you. Have you told her that you love her—or have you, as usual, left her to guess that you do? I leave you to think on it."

The struggle was brief, love overcame pride. But Adrian's decision to search for Juliane was thwarted before it could be put into action.

Reentering the room excitedly as Adrian was about to leave, Cavilón said, "A messenger has just arrived with word from one of our men. He believes he may have located the kidnappers. We are to meet him at the Oaks this evening."

"Good. Action is what we need." Adrian rubbed his hands in anticipation.

"My lord," interrupted Holdt. "There are two, er, gentlemen asking to see you."

"Did they give their names or mention their business?"

"One said he was Squire Preston; the other is . . . questionable. They said their business was private."

"The squire? Ah, the magistrate. Take him to my study. I will join them in a few moments," ordered Lord Adrian. To Cavilón he said, "I will be back. We will lay our plans as soon as I finish with them. Wait for me."

As Lord Adrian entered his study, the squire and his companion stood, ill at ease.

"I understand you wish to see me," Adrian said as he stood before them.

"Ah, yes," squirmed the squire.

"What is it that you wish of me?"

"If you will let me speak, m'lord," the second man said, stepping forward.

"As you will."

"There was an unpleasant incident some weeks back involving the deaths of a postilion and an abigail." He paused.

Lord Adrian said nothing, merely seating himself behind his desk.

"The squire, here," he jerked his head toward the uncomfortable-looking man, he says he talked with your man at . . ." He paused once more, removing a small book from inside his coat and thumbing through the pages. "He talked with your man, Mallatt, at a farmer's cottage—Jove Foster's. Is this true?"

"Yes."

"Mr. Foster said you, your wife, two children, and valet stumbled into their farmyard during a heavy snowstorm. You were injured?" He looked at Lord Adrian who nodded, then continued. "The day before you departed, there was an attempt to abduct the boy—André?"

Again Lord Adrian nodded—not certain of the direction this questioning was taking.

"This is all true?" the man asked, evidently unsatisfied by Adrian's nod.

Lord Adrian rose and walked around his desk slowly. "Squire, perhaps you could explain all these questions."

"We don't, ah, we don't want to cause you no trouble, your lordship—but I am magistrate."

"I should explain, Lord Tretain. I am Michael

216

Dougherty—a runner from London," said the second man.

"A runner? What do you need with me. How can I be of help?"

"There are certain irregularities revolving around the murders. This concerns your wife and must be cleared up."

The slight inflection on wife caught Lord Adrian's attention. "I quite agree. Be on with it then."

"Through our investigation, we have learned that the coach and murdered postilion were hired a day's journey from South Hampton by a woman calling herself Lady Juliane Perrill. She had with her two small children and an abigail—the description of that abigail and the murdered woman match. Is it not odd, Lord Tretain, that you suddenly have a wife and two children, although we can find no record of your ever being married?"

Squire Preston coughed at Dougherty's bluntness. "We do not mean to imply that you are involved in the murders, my lord. But you can see the need for questions."

Lord Adrian's cold stare silenced him. It had not occurred to him that the squire would bring in outsiders to handle the crime. "I am certain this can all be explained satisfactorily. Won't you gentlemen be seated—something to drink perhaps?"

The squire acquiesced happily; Dougherty declined.

"The facts are simple. My wife and I married in France. She and her maid traveled ahead while I finished a business venture. We did not wish news of the marriage to reach my mother before we did, so she used her family name. We met traveling to Trees. I

217

had an accident with my phaeton, the snowstorm developed, and the postilion and abigail refused to go on." Stopping, he poured himself a drink. "I could have my valet come and corroborate all this."

"Not necessary," assured the squire hurriedly, as Dougherty frowned.

"As I said, they refused to go on and turned back. We were very shocked to learn of their deaths."

"But, what of the attempted abduction?" asked Dougherty.

"I am a rich man. Someone hoped to hold the boy for ransom. We have taken precautions since then."

"That clears it up, eh, Dougherty? Let's be getting on. His lordship doesn't need us taking up his time."

"I am happy I could oblige you," said Lord Adrian dryly.

"You go on, Squire. I know you are anxious to return to your family. Would you mind, Lord Tretain, if I stayed and talked with your wife?" asked the runner.

Lord Adrian assessed the man. He would likely be more trouble away than near. At least within the house they could keep a watch on him. "By all means. You are welcome to stay. I will have Holdt show you a room, and you can visit with Lady Tretain later."

"That would be very satisfactory."

"Good." He opened the door. "Holdt, show Mr. Dougherty to a room. Squire," he said, turning to the other, "may I see you to your horse?"

"No, no. Not necessary, Lord Tretain. Hope we haven't inconvenienced you."

"Think nothing of it. Just doing your duty. I understand." Having come into the hall, he added, "Farewell then."

"Good day, your lordship."

The two men shook hands and went their separate ways. Lord Adrian headed for the small salon.

"What has kept you?" Count Cavilón greeted him.

"An added complication. We are half rid of it, but the remaining half may prove more tenacious—certainly more troublesome—a runner."

"A runner? One of your English authorities—here? But why? How?"

"The good squire who is magistrate where the murders occurred sent for him. Dougherty by name. He became suspicious of . . . details. Blast! Damnation. I had hoped to keep the entire matter silent. You and Mallatt are the only ones who actually know Juliane and I were not married until last night. It was all perfectly innocent, but if this gets out. . . . We must find those men—quickly."

"Calm yourself, *mon ami,*" soothed Cavilón. "Remember, our friend may have what we need. Shall I meet him alone?"

"That may be necessary unless I can convince Juliane . . . Juliane, I had started to find her to talk . . ." A clock sounded. "Well, it is time for luncheon. I will talk with her after that. We shall see what will be."

Adrian and the count headed for the dining room.

"Ah, Mr. Dougherty—are you comfortably settled?" asked Lord Adrian, as the runner joined them for luncheon.

"Yes, m'lord. Thank you."

Holdt came to Lord Adrian's chair and whispered,

"Lady Tretain wishes me to tell you she shall take luncheon in her room. She will not eat at the same table as 'that person.' "

"That is fine, Holdt. Do you know where our other guests are?"

"I believe most have kept to their rooms, my lord."

"Probably not up to snuff after last night. It was late after all."

Mr. Dougherty's presence had a subduing effect on those who did sit to luncheon. It was a quiet and quick affair.

"If you will excuse me," Lord Adrian rose.

"When may I speak with Lady Tretain?" asked Dougherty, also rising.

"I am certain she will be recovered sufficiently by this evening. Amuse yourself until then with what you can find. Look over the grounds—the gardens are quite extensive—whatever interests you," answered Lord Adrian, leaving before the runner could object or ask further questions. He made a mental note to instruct the staff about Mr. Dougherty.

Lord Adrian next went to Juliane's room, entering without pausing to allow time for her to answer his knock. Finding the room empty, he sent for Bess, and looked around the room while he waited, absentmindedly closing the jewelry case he saw open on her dressing table.

"What is it, my lord," puffed Bess, winded from her run up two flights of stairs.

"Where is Lady Juliane?"

"I don't know, my lord. I helped her into a riding habit early this morning and she dismissed me—said I wasn't needed," said Bess with an injured air.

"Did she say where she was going or when she would return?"

"No, my lord. It was strange of her—asking for the valise and all."

"What valise?" he asked, alarmed.

"Lady Juliane wished me to fetch the smallest valise in the house. I have no idea why."

"That will be all," he dismissed her curtly.

"Is everything all right, my lord?"

"Of course," came the answer as he slammed through the passageway into his room.

Mallatt started guiltily at the sight of his lord.

"What is wrong with you?" snapped Lord Adrian.

Holding out his hand, Mallatt slowly opened his fingers. Lord Adrian stepped closer and reached for the rings.

"She has gone," he said hollowly. Walking to the bureau, he laid them down.

"We don't know that, my lord, or the reason, if she has," countered Mallatt.

"Was anything else out of place?"

"Her ladyship has taken one of your pistols. She went through the bureau drawer hurriedly and it was not closed properly," he offered in explanation.

"My God!" Adrian rubbed his forehead. "I am going to Cavilón's room. Try to learn if she has actually left and then join us there. There is a runner in the house—Dougherty. Avoid him."

"Yes, my lord. Should I have our horses readied?"

"No. We have to sort this out carefully before we move. Quickly now."

Striding through the halls, Lord Adrian heard Cavilón's voice coming from the library. Slowing his pace drastically, he sauntered in to find Lord and Lady Stern, Sir Percival, and Lady Cecile visiting with his friend. Out of the corner of his eye, he spied Dougherty lounging in the background.

"We heard Lady Juliane is not well," said Lady Stern. "Is it something serious?"

"No, no. Too much excitement. She will join us later," he smiled.

"I am pleased to hear that," tossed in Dougherty, who had risen and joined the group. "I have learned some most interesting information."

"Is that for certain?" asked Lord Adrian.

"Everything is interesting about Lady Juliane," Lady Cecile threw in cattily.

Lord Adrian tossed her a scornful look, and approaching Cavilón, slapped him on the back. "I am sorry we must leave you all for a time, but there is a matter that must be tended to and only my friend here can assist me."

"Not another of your wild wagers?" asked Lord Stern.

Saying nothing to discredit the idea, Lord Adrian tossed out easily, "Cousin Percy, won't you see to the entertainment of my guests? Excuse us." He guided Cavilón through the door. Seeing Dougherty move after them, he shoved the count none too gently through the first door he came to and motioned him to be quiet.

"We won't be alone long if I know that man."

"What is this about?"

"Juliane is gone—Mallatt should be getting to your room soon." He looked into the corridor. "Follow me."

They hurried down long hallways, pausing at the door to the count's room.

"That was the most unusual tour of your house I have ever had, Adrian. You should treat more of your guests to it," said Cavilón, brushing dust from his sleeves.

Lord Adrian grimaced at him. "Here is Mallatt—let's go in."

The door shut behind the three. Cavilón looked to Adrian and Lord Adrian looked to Mallatt.

"Lady Juliane took Belle out early this morning. She had a small valise with her and her cloak as well. The groom said she intimated she would be back in a short time but there has been no sign of her."

"Do you suppose she . . ." Cavilón began.

"Yes. She probably decided to find the children on her own. It would be just like her," Adrian answered.

"But what about Dougherty? He seems to be set upon speaking with her."

"I know. That would involve telling him far more than I desire to. Something I refuse to do, in fact. It is my fault that she is in this position," Lord Adrian swore.

"My lord, if I may make a suggestion," offered Mallatt. "I and a handful of men can look over the countryside for Lady Juliane this afternoon while you keep Mr. Dougherty occupied. I believe he has asked to speak with Lady Tretain. Her ladyship, your mother, my lord, is indeed Lady Tretain, and I feel she could give Mr. Dougherty a most interesting time of it—enough time to allow you and the count to get away and find Lady Juliane if we are not successful."

Cavilón nodded. "If we fail, you can always explain matters to him."

"I can explain matters?" quizzed Lord Adrian with a cocked eyebrow.

Endless as the yards of tulle making up the ruching on Lady Cecile's gown was the day. The longer rays of the setting sun streaming through the salon windows caught Lord Adrian's attention. In France he had spent many such lingering days but, having never been quite so personally involved before, he found the pleasantries and inanimate activities of this day a sore trial. Fortunately, he displayed only a slight sarcasm and this was laid to his changeable temperament.

"We must change if we are to dine on time," Lord Adrian threw out. "We keep country hours here, Mr. Dougherty. I do hope it isn't too bothersome."

"Of course not, Lord Tretain. I do hope I'll have the pleasure of Lady Tretain's company at dinner."

"Till later." Adrian escaped with a sigh. The man had become like a leech. Louís should have returned by now.

A short white later Cavilón walked in, shaking his head. "There is no sign of her. We did learn she had stopped at a cottage or two early in the day asking if the people had seen the children. Then nothing."

His brow furrowed with concern, Lord Adrian paced.

"They are still searching," his friend tried to console him. "She may return on her own."

Shaking his head, Lord Adrian said, "The nights

are still severe. She has only a cloak. What if she takes a deathly chill?"

"Come, Adrian. If you will forgive me, Lady Juliane is as healthy as *le cheval de proverbe* and of quick intellect."

"Which she is not using!"

"We had better dress for dinner. Have you attended to Dougherty's interview?" asked Cavilón, with a smile.

"No. I had best hurry to Mother's apartments. What explanation I will give for asking her to do this is beyond me."

"Ah, Adrian. You are doing it 'too brown' as you Englishmen are fond of saying. I have yet to see a tale beyond your means. True, yours are sometimes a bit *fantastique* but they are manageable, nevertheless," said the count, laughing.

"But never so close to my heart," said Adrian grimly.

Michael Dougherty felt something was very out of sorts at Trees. His reception had been usual enough and his treatment, to be truthful, was far more pleasant than he had received in some of the gentry's homes he had visited on occasions of business. Lord Adrian was just a bit on edge, it seemed to him, but he liked the man. There was an air on the part of some of the servants that bespoke unease, especially in his presence, as if there had been an occurrence he would be interested in. It was odd that he had neither seen nor heard any sign of the two children. On such a lovely day he would have expected their nurse to arrange an outing.

"Mr. Dougherty," coughed Holdt. "Lady Tretain will see you now. Follow me." He led the runner up the stairs and through corridors, finally halting before an imposing set of doors. "Her ladyship awaits," he said, opening the doors for the runner. Dougherty passed through and Holdt pulled them shut.

The candlelight in the room was soft and Mr. Dougherty scanned the room keenly. He would not have thought that Lady Tretain had been at Trees long enough to add such a personal mark to the decorations. She apparently had in this sitting room. And where was her ladyship? Walking to the center of the room, he cleared his throat loudly.

"Mr. Dougherty?" came the question from behind a large screen to one side.

"It is, m'lady."

"Please be seated by the fire. I will be with you shortly."

The runner seated himself, thinking how different voices generally are from what one expects.

A half hour later, Mr. Dougherty cleared his throat again—loudly.

"Just a few more moments, my good man. I have not been well today."

Twenty minutes later, his patience expended, he rose. The sound of his action brought a movement behind the screen.

"You young people," complained Lady Tretain, coming grandly into view, "are always rushing."

Dougherty stood, mouth agape, for a few seconds. Then he gained his composure. "I am sorry, but I believed I was brought to see Lady Tretain."

"And so you were. No one has ever asked to see my

226

marriage lines all these years past—but I can produce them, I assure you."

"I did not mean, I apologize, m'lady. It . . ."

"I can understand your confusion." She waved a hand elegantly at him, then stood silent.

"May I ask . . ."

"Why that is what I understood you wished—to ask questions. It would seem senseless for you to disturb me and then not ask them, would it not?" she asked, enjoying herself thoroughly.

"It is my understanding . . . Lord Tretain has a wife . . ." stuttered the runner, trying to remain calm.

"Of course he did," Lady Tretain said, cutting in before he could complete his question. "How do you suppose we came by the present heir?" she asked exasperatedly.

"That is who I am speaking of—Lord Adrian Tretain—and his wife—Lady Juliane."

"Well, for heaven's sake . . . Why don't you make yourself clear?"

Dougherty stared at her, waiting for more. When no further information was forthcoming, he asked, "Am I not to be allowed to see her then?"

"No one is preventing you, but then, I am not certain where she has gone to."

"Lady Juliane is not at Trees?" the runner asked, all his suspicions aroused.

"No, nothing of the sort. It is just that she flits about so—to the nursery, to the salon, to her room."

"She is very nervous then?" asked the runner with satisfaction.

"No, the calmest woman I have ever met. Mr.

Dougherty, could I not interest you in a small glass of . . . refreshment?" asked Lady Tretain, deeming the timing appropriate.

Dougherty scratched his head. "Not my usual habit, you understand, m'lady. But a spot wouldn't hurt just now."

"I am certain it would not. Let us be seated. Satter," she called. "Glasses for the gentleman and myself."

Satter entered from a side door carrying a silver tray with a bottle of sherry and two glasses. The glasses did a merry dance upon the tray as she nervously served them.

Dougherty noticed this and thought it odd but, as her ladyship made no comment, he dismissed it.

Lady Tretain removed the stopper from the decanter and poured the two glasses full. Indicating for the runner to pick one up, she chose the remaining one and raised it. "Shall we say, to your health. You do look a bit tired." Smiling, she raised the glass to her lips.

"To yours, m'lady." He quaffed the drink down.

Lady Tretain lowered her glass without having taken a sip. "Sherry should never be gulped, my man. When one does it that way, strange things happen to one."

"Such as . . ."

"Why, I am told one becomes sleepy—now there you are yawning. You must remember never to gulp, mustn't you, Mr. Dougherty. Mr. Dougherty?

"My, my. Satter," she called once more. "My guest has found my conversation most boring. Would you fetch Holdt and some others to remove him?"

Watching the men carry the runner from the room, Lady Tretain puzzled over the brief explanation Adrian had given her.

The children were missing, Lady Juliane was off somewhere searching for them, and now he and the count were looking for her. A runner was not needed in all this confusion.

Surely, she asked herself, one could get into trouble meddling with a runner. But it was only a harmless sleeping potion; Mr. Dougherty would get a good night's rest and he couldn't be angry with her for that. I do hope Adrian is pleased, she thought with a smile. I do believe this is the most fun I've had in years.

But her thoughts took a darker turn. Were the children and Juliane safe? What was happening?

22

Darkness had fallen an hour past. Lord Adrian, Count Cavilón, and Mallatt arrived at the Oaks, an ale house which also served as an inn, just as a group of local men left it. They remained in the darkness as the men passed close by, their Thoroughbred horses the only evidence of their high station in life. Mallatt had secured clothing that no one who had attended the ball could ever be convinced either the count or Lord Adrian would deign to touch, much less wear. Such garb suited well their purposes on this evening, however.

Leaving the horses in Mallatt's hands, they entered the public room. Their appearance drew little attention from the motley group assembled. An equally ragged fellow at a table to the rear beckoned to them. Ordering mugs of ale, they joined him.

Nodding a silent greeting, the three men waited

until the ale had been served and the innkeeper was out of hearing.

"What news do you have for us?" asked Lord Adrian.

"It is as you thought. They are using the empty cottages and huts on your estate. They have been moving every few days, and separately. As you know," the man frowned apologetically, "we lost three of them last night. The fourth, however, we have kept in our sights. We expect him to lead us back to the others."

"What do you mean he'll lead you? Have you no idea where they are?" asked the count.

"Unfortunately we have only a fair idea. Wait, here's Tom."

A fourth man pulled a chair to the table. After glancing cautiously about, he said, "The coves have settled for the night—or so we think. Can't be too certain of anything these frogs do. There are two men keepin' watch till we can get there."

"Did you see anyone with them—two small children, the girl, a young woman?" asked Lord Adrian, reaching across the table to take hold of the man's arm.

"Nay, m'lord, I'm sorry to say—none of them."

"Let us ride and see where this is," said the count, rising. "We shall decide what is to be done from that point."

The others rose also, tossed their coin on the table, and strode from the inn.

A half-score miles away, the two men left to watch the hut were engaged in earnest conversation.

"Who can that be? What? A woman. What would a woman be about this time a night? And alone!"

"She must be with 'em."

"We've seen no sign o' the likes of her before—it's too dark to tell who she might be."

"See—goin' right to the door. Look . . ."

"I tell you, she ain't with 'em. See, one is creepin' up behind her—and, look, another is gettin' her mount. Somethin' funny goin' on here."

"They're takin' her in. Must be a local wench— couldn't be of the Quality. She'd a fainted dead away if she was," said the one with utter certainty.

Unknown to him, Lady Juliane had never been closer to fainting in all her life. Once confronted, only the cultivated voice and polite manner of the apparent leader eased her fears slightly. Deeming nothing to be gained from a struggle but the loss of her dignity, she entered as bade unprotestingly.

From what she could discern in the light of the single flickering candle, no one had been in the hut for years. The dress and manner of the men was foreign.

As the door shut, the three men broke into rapid French, confirming Lady Juliane's guess as to their origins. They must be the men who had been following them. But where were Alva and the children?

The refined man the others referred to as *Mon seigneur* silenced them. Making a leg, he said in English, "Please forgive my men. Their manners have been sadly neglected. It was most obliging of you to join us, Lady Perrill. You have saved us much time."

"Then you have the children?" she asked eagerly.

"*Mais, oui, madame.*"

232

"Where are they—not here?" She looked about. It did not seem possible that they could be held here unknown to her.

"Do not trouble yourself about where they are. As of the present, they are well. Let us hope you can help them remain so," he finished tauntingly.

"I must see them. They will have been frightened."

"You will." At a sign, the three men melted into the darkness as the fourth snuffed the candle.

Lady Juliane felt her hand gripped and dared not draw back. If only she could get to her horse and the pistol.

"Be still, *madame*. It would be such a shame to silence you."

Outside, the men watching were confounded. The three who had left the hut could be heard riding off, each in a different direction.

"Now what do we do?"

"I'll stay here. Lem said their lordships would join us. You get your mount. Follow the two that haven't left yet."

As the sounds of the three horses grew faint, the man holding onto Lady Juliane tugged at her to follow. She was thankful for the split skirt of her riding habit as he forced her out the hut through a rear window. Brush and branches caught at her skirt but he pulled her on ruthlessly. Bumping into him as he halted suddenly, she saw that they had come upon his horse.

Balking at first when he indicated she was to mount, Lady Juliane quickly changed her mind as he grabbed her about the waist. Somehow she contrived to get into the saddle and settle her skirt decently as he led the horse off.

When they were some distance from the hut, he vaulted onto the mount behind her. Lady Juliane cringed as he reached around her and took hold of the reins he had laid across the mane. At first the horse walked, but soon he prodded it into a gallop.

Back at the hut, the two watchers still waited for some sign of life.

"I don't like this—they should have left by now. There's not been a light since the others left."

"Perhaps they already left."

"Gads! Not again. It's too late to follow any of the others. What should we do?"

"You had better go around the hut and check. We know the direction he came from. It's logical he'll head back that way. See if you can spot anything—if you do, follow it. I better stay here and wait. Come back if you find their nest."

In the meantime, Lord Adrian, Count Cavilón, and the others rode steadily. Tom halted and signaled them to dismount a short distance from where he had left the others. With the mounts secured to various brush, he led the way, crouching low. His hoot was answered as a man emerged from the darkness. He and Tom spoke briefly; then Tom turned to Lord Adrian.

"We are at a standstill, m'lord. They have departed with a woman, perhaps your wife, who either blundered onto them or joined them. Her mount is still here."

"Have it brought here. What is being done?"

"Davey is followin' the man and woman that left together. He will return here."

The mare was led before Lord Adrian. "That's Belle all right," he confirmed to Cavilón. "It is my wife they have."

Two hours later an impatient Lord Adrian had worn a path in the grass. The others huddled together for warmth. Suddenly all heads cocked at a sound—a horse approaching at a deadly gallop.

They remained hidden until it became clear the rider was heading for their hiding place. The horse plunged to a halt in their midst.

"Did you find them?"

"Aye. We had better hurry. The man and woman I followed have gone to a farm. There is a coach and four all ready to travel there. I saw two of the others before I left. I figure they will depart as soon as the other one arrives."

These words mobilized the group. Horses were brought forth. "Take the mare, Davey," ordered Lord Adrian. "She is fresh."

The switch was made and they were off, the moon lighting the way.

"Time to be departing, *ma belle*," ordered the leader of the band, entering the farm cottage.

"Where are you taking us?" Lady Juliane demanded. She held André while Alva clutched Leora.

"Far enough from here to be safe until we get what we came after."

"Why not tell us what you want?" she pleaded.

His bitter laugh startled her. "As if you did not know."

"But I do not!"

"Bah! Why else did you go to Rouen? They sent for you. If you are not careful, your end will be like your sister's."

Lady Juliane tightened her hold on André's hand. She had never expected to come face to face with Judith's murderer.

"Move now. We waste too much time," he commanded, grabbing André and shoving him toward the door.

The toy soldier in André's hand fell. As he reached to pick it up, the man stepped on it, grinding it beneath his foot.

Lady Juliane walked slowly to the spot. Exchanging looks for several moments, the man cursed and stepped away. Lady Juliane stooped and picked up the crumpled toy and handed it to André. "Put it into your pocket—we will have it repaired." Taking his hand, she led the way out of the cottage. Alva followed with Leora.

They hurried across the farmyard to the waiting coach and were roughly pushed in.

"Voici," said one of the men, and he tossed in Lady Juliane's valise and another containing the children's belongings. Juliane grabbed hers hurriedly and stashed it behind her. With the pistol a secure bump against her back, she attempted to quiet the other's whimperings.

"What will become of us?" cried Alva. "I'll never see me Mum and Da again."

"Have faith—Lord Adrian will not let us come to harm," she assured Alva, not daring to question her belief in the statement.

*   *   *

Lord Adrian halted his group. Cavilón and Mallatt edged up beside him. "Davey, how far is it?"

"Just a short piece now."

"As I thought. They most likely will have left. What is your guess as to their destination?" he asked Cavilón.

"There is not much choice for them. I would guess London or South Hampton—perhaps Dover—to be their goal. Any way they wish to go, they must use the same road for several miles."

"My thought exactly. Did you say you saw all of them?"

"Only one was missing, m'lord. And he couldn't have been far, because they all left the hut at the same time."

"Let's cross country then. We can get ahead and surprise them. They should not be expecting us."

"Is this wise?" asked Cavilón. "Perhaps some of us should go on to the farm."

"No, we will risk it."

"You are usually right, Adrian. Let's not waste time."

Pounding over the treacherous dark landscape, Mallatt wondered how he had ever concluded that Lady Juliane would be a calming influence on his lordship's life. His lord was now safely married, but here he was on still another wild and dangerous adventure. This had better be the last time, he thought to himself as he followed the swerving horses before him.

An hour's ride brought them to their destination.

"We should have little trouble. They will believe

us to be highwaymen. Mallatt, take Tom and go further up the road in case they get by us. Louís, take Lem and cover this side of the road. The rest of you, come with me to the other side. Have your pistols ready. Remember those within the coach and take careful aim." He looked around at the men in the group. "Dead men can do no harm."

Cavilón nodded and reined away. Soon there was no sign of their presence. The waiting began once more.

Sometime later the pounding of hooves caught their attention.

"Davey, is that the coach you saw?" whispered Lord Adrian.

"Aye, m'lord. I remember the front team—them white feet ain't common."

As Lord Adrian hoped, indeed prayed, it seemed all of the men were outside the coach. Two were on it and the other two rode alongside.

"They get one chance," Adrian muttered. Spurring his mount from the brush, he called out. "Halt. Stop if you value your lives."

There was a momentary check in the coach's progress, then bedlam broke loose as shouts, gunshots, and men's cries erupted amid the thundering of hooves and whinnying of horses.

Inside the lurching coach, Lady Juliane tightened her grip on the wall strap and dug into the valise she had managed to open earlier. Fumbling desperately, her hand came in contact with the pistol.

The gentleman who had joined them in the coach was cursing and waving his own pistol about as he strove to keep his balance. He called repeatedly to his men but none answered.

Outside in the dust left by the bolting coach's teams lay the two riders and one of the men who had been atop it. The night's blackness hid the quickly spreading stains beneath them. Lem had halted and was making sure of the work.

The remainder of Lord Adrian's group pursued the coach, now running wildly out of control. As Mallatt and Tom caught hold of the teams and were slowing them, the others drew alongside.

Lord Adrian sprung from his mount, shouting "Juliane!" as the coach was jerked to a halt. Wresting open the coach door, he was greeted by the thunderous explosions of two pistols.

Upon hearing Lord Adrian's voice, Lady Juliane had felt her heart rise. Then, perceiving the gentleman across from her aim at the direction of Adrian's call, she raised her pistol from behind her back and discharged it a fraction before he discharged his. Her aim was true; she sat frozen as the gentleman sprawled forward, his blood spurting. The next moment the opposite coach door was jerked open and four pistols intruded, furthering the hysterics of Alva and the children. The body was roughly pulled out, thumping soddenly to the ground.

A familiar voice commanded, "Lady Juliane, give me the pistol. It is over now."

Only as Leora's wailing penetrated her mind did life come back to Juliane.

"Cavilón," she breathed, releasing her frozen grip on the gun. She looked blankly at the open door nearest her, and then her body finally obeyed her mind: She screamed, "Adrian!" and jumped from the coach. Dropping to the ground, she knelt beside the prone figure of her husband.

23

"Is he . . . ?" Julian asked fearfully.

"No, he is alive, but I can't tell the extent of the wound. It is in the shoulder. Do you have anything to staunch the bleeding?"

"Alva," Lady Juliane called, rising and turning toward the coach. "Quickly—one of Leora's nappies."

The article was hurriedly handed to her. She knelt and pressed it to the wound. "What of the others?" she asked as Count Cavilón knelt at her side.

"All dead but for the coachman, and I do not think his life will be long. We must get Adrian to Trees." He motioned to the two men behind him. Between them they managed to get the earl into the coach.

"Mallatt, handle the ribbons. Lem, care for the coachman—we want answers from him. Tom, fetch the surgeon to Trees. The rest of you collect our friends and follow."

"Aye, m'lord," echoed all.

Mallatt whipped the team up even as Cavilón stepped into the coach.

Lord Adrian lay unconscious in Juliane's arms, her hand pressing the pad tightly to his wound. "Another," she snapped as she felt the warmth of blood seeping through.

Cavilón knelt on the coach floor. "Put his shoulders in your lap. You will be able to staunch the blood more easily. I will help."

The coach rolled on endlessly. Infrequent glimpses of Adrian's face in the moonlight fed Juliane's worst fears for his life, for her happiness, which she now knew lay only with him.

Finally there was a last lurch and Mallett's shouts announced that they were at home at last. A sleepy-eyed Holdt was jerked from drowsiness as Cavilón handed out the blood-spattered children. "Quickly," Cavilón ordered. "The earl is wounded."

The remainder of the night was a blur to Juliane. Lady Tretain took charge. The arrival of the surgeon signaled their removal from Adrian's chamber.

"Bess has a bath drawn for you. We can do nothing but await the surgeon's judgment," Lady Tretain told her. "The children have been given the fright of their lives. You must make yourself presentable and go to them."

"But I . . ." Juliane turned to Adrian's door.

"To your bath. We will be told how he does." With a wave of her hand, the countess motioned Juliane away.

* * *

Morning brought a false calm. The surgeon had departed with assurances that the shot had been removed, and although his lordship had lost a lot of blood, his recovery was certain, barring infection. Leaving a potion and instructions, he went his way, promising to return by evening to check his patient.

Juliane had seen to the children and then sat with Lord Adrian. She snuffed out the candles as full light flooded the room. He stirred. Taking his hand, she spoke softly, soothingly. Adrian lay still for some time, then stirred once more. Muttering, he began tossing about.

"Mallatt," Juliane called. "We must hold him still. The wound will open. Adrian," she urged, "rest. You are at Trees."

"Trees?" he mumbled. "Can't be at Trees. I'm not bosky? Must find my angel."

"Lie still now. You were shot. If you keep moving, you will start the bleeding again. Hush now, lie quietly."

"Angel—my angel," he struggled to open his eyes. "Lost her."

"No one is lost." Juliane spoke softly, tears coming to her eyes. If only he were to speak so of her. Feeling him relax in her hold, she blinked back her tears. His eyes were open. His feverish gaze was neither hard nor cold as it met hers. "Angel," he sighed. "You . . . came . . . back."

Mallatt deemed his presence unnecessary and quietly left the chamber.

"You were wounded, Adrian. The man in the coach—he shot you," she managed.

He closed his eyes tiredly and shook his head slowly. "Were you . . . harmed?"

"No," she answered simply. "The children were frightened witless but are well now. André has asked after you."

Lord Adrian smiled weakly. "What happened to the one who shot me?"

"He is dead."

"Cavilón," he sighed. "Always dependable."

"You must sleep now."

"I must speak with Louís—he must take care of Dougherty."

"When you awake."

Closing his eyes, Adrian relaxed. Soon he was breathing deeply, rhythmically.

Lady Tretain entered her son's chamber quietly. "How is he?"

Leaving her chair, Juliane whispered, "He is sleeping peacefully. Can you sit with him? I must see Count Cavilón."

"The count is having a rather 'stimulating' morn. I imagine he will want . . . Well, let him explain." Lady Tretain took Juliane's hand and led her into the hall. "Mallatt," she said to the valet hovering by the door, "sit with him. We shall be back directly. You," she instructed Juliane, "go directly to my sitting room. I will extract the count." She smiled conspiritorially, then moved regally down the hall.

Count Cavilón joined Juliane in Lady Tretain's sitting room just minutes later.

"Your thoughts are deep, my lady," Count Cavilón said, walking slowly to Juliane.

She unsuccessfully tried to force a smile.

"We have little time," he sighed.

"What do you mean?" she asked, puzzled.

Briefly he explained about the runner—Dougherty. When she seemed to recognize the man, he asked, "Do you know the man?"

"No, Adrian mumbled something about you having to take care of a Dougherty."

"I suppose he thinks it *juste* I am saddled with the task of smoothing things over since he is unable to."

"What trouble can Dougherty cause?"

"Much, but he won't. We will let him take the credit for last night's work. He wishes your statement and then will go."

"But what can I tell him?"

"Adrian has told him you were married in France. Simply tell of going to Rouen, what you found there—mention that you planned to meet Adrian at Trees. Have no fear. I will guide you and will interrupt if necessary."

"Thank you. Adrian is fortunate to have a friend such as you." She paused once more. "Did you learn what the men wanted?"

"*Oui*—the wounded man spoke of many things before he died. It seems La Croix . . ."

"La Croix," Juliane interrupted him. "Then it was André's father who was responsible."

"No. A cousin. André is now Baron La Croix. I will explain this all later. We must go to Dougherty now."

Awakening with a start, Lady Juliane relaxed as she realized she was safe at Trees. It had been an interminable ten days since that long and terrible night in which Adrian had been wounded. He had awakened with a clear head three days after the incident; an invisible barrier had slipped between them. There were few excuses to go to him once he was out of danger and he had not sent for her. She rose and pulled on her wrapper, her eyes on the closed connecting doors. How long would this go on? Was there no hope?

"Good morn, my lady. You look well rested. Lady Tretain said you were to breakfast before you did anything." Bess held out the tray. "I wouldn't be surprised if her ladyship popped in to see if you were eating. They say Lord Tretain is much improved this morn. He ate a hearty breakfast." Bess prattled on as her mistress ate.

Her meal finished, Juliane dressed carefully in the green watered-silk gown that Adrian had chosen for her long ago. Her coiffure arranged, she walked about her chamber fretfully, wondering if she should go to Adrian or await his summons.

Deep in thought, she jumped at a knock on her connecting door. She rushed to it, fear and longing upon her features.

Count Cavilón stepped back as she pulled it open. "Why," he said, taking her hand, "what has upset you?" Then, noticing her eyes straining for what lay beyond the end of the passageway, he laughed gently. "You think he is worse? No, he is so well recovered that he is complaining of the lack of your company."

Forcing herself to walk slowly, Juliane went to the bedside. Lord Adrian's eyes danced, then darkened at her quiet demeanour. "You did not wish to see me?" he asked quietly.

Juliane felt a slow blush begin. Did she dare say

what she felt? "I am . . . pleased . . . that you are so improved, my lord. What is it?" she asked, leaning forward with concern as he frowned.

"You are being unfair."

"Unfair?!"

"Yes, lean closer, please," he whispered. When she did so, he kissed her—causing her to blush fiercely as Cavilón looked on smiling. "I told you I keep my word."

"You are incorrigible," she stated with a half-hidden smile, shaking her head and sitting in the chair Cavilón brought to the bedside.

"Louís, why do you not make things clear for Juliane?" Adrian reached for her hand.

"I will try to keep this *simple*," Cavilón smiled as he gazed at the pair.

"Baron La Croix left his home to try and protect his family. He had reports that his cousin—Eutin Renoit—was planning to use the unrest caused by the *revolutionaires* to make himself heir to the title and possessor of the family's wealth. The baron urged his wife to come with him—even to flee to England, but she refused. Eutin was responsible for her death. He then caught the baron and demanded he hand over the La Croix emeralds, but something happened—the baron was killed. Eutin learned of your visit, the children's survival, and began his pursuit, certain you had the jewels.

"Cora was killed because she did not have them and knew nothing. The attempts to take André were made to force you to hand over the jewels."

Juliane shook her head. It was fantastic; she had had no inkling.

"Eutin failed in more than one way," continued the count. It was he who shot Adrian. One more thing you should realize, my lady," his face saddened. "With the mob ruling France, André's title is useless, his estates gone."

There was silence, then Juliane asked. "Yours also?"

"I was prepared," Cavilón nodded. "I was prepared." He passed a hand across his face, erasing the sadness. "As I told Adrian, Dougherty has cleared the incident. There should be no further trouble." Smiling, he ended, "I bid you *adieu*. Lady Cecile has promised me a most diverting journey—I am to escort her home." With a raised eyebrow and a gracious leg, he left them.

Juliane became conscious of Adrian's grip on her hand, of the warmth his touch brought her. Searching for words, she thrust back those she wished to speak and said, "The children—I must find Uncle Thedford for them. He has named André his heir."

"I have had word on him," Adrian spoke slowly, releasing her hand.

"You knew I meant to go to him?" she asked in disbelief.

"Not exactly, but it seemed the most likely thing. You mentioned an uncle on your first night here.

"I fear your plans are hopeless," he continued. "There is no estate. The reason your family never had anything to do with him was that he was more than slightly daft and had lost everything long before André was born. An old family retainer kept him until he died a few years ago."

Juliane studied the quilting on the coverlet. What would she do? Where would they go if . . . ?

248

"I have said I would adopt the children—do you object so?" His voice throbbed with emotion.

Her eyes flew to his, her heart pounding.

"My lord, my lord," Mallatt scampered in excitedly. "You won't believe it—it can hardly be credited. Look," he held out one of André's toy soldiers for them to see. "I was straightening it and it broke. See what fell out!" With a shake of the toy several green stones tumbled onto the bed.

"The emeralds," breathed Juliane.

"The other soldiers are full of them," he continued, then, noticing that the two before him had eyes only for each other, he added, "We will see to this later, my lord. Of course, my lord." He bowed and hurriedly withdrew.

"How could I have doubted you?" Juliane breathed.

"I could have explained I was an agent for the ministry . . ."

Fingers brushed his lips to silence. "There is no need to tell me now."

He caught her hand once more. "Do you love me? *Can* you love me? Every moment since I regained my senses I have feared you would leave—that is why I dared not send for you. I love you so."

"Oh, Adrian, I have longed to hear . . ."

No more was said as his lips claimed her lips— claiming her heart as well.

"My angel," he breathed, "my own." Drinking in the love glowing in her eyes, his happiness was complete. "On the dressing chest . . ."

Juliane gave a puzzled glance toward it. The rings he had given her lay upon a tray.

"Will you not wear them—always?" His ardour caused his voice to tremble.

She rose and retrieved them. Sitting beside the earl, she asked saucily. "Will you not replace them . . . my lord?"

He slipped the rings on her finger, saying sternly, "You know I shall have to break you of this formality in address."

"I know . . . my lord," Juliane answered, happily surrendering to his fervent embrace.

The unforgettable story of a woman's search for the father she had never known.

THE ADMIRAL'S DAUGHTER
Victoria Fyodorova and Haskel Frankel

It began in Moscow during World War II—a story of secret trysts and midnight arrests. It became the story of a love that leapt the boundaries of fear, of language, of international power and politics to see a beautiful woman reunited with her father at last.

"One of the most thrilling, ingenious and frightening spy stories I've ever read, and all the more powerful because it's true."
—*The Hollywood Reporter*

"A book that you cannot put down."—*New York Post*

A Dell Book $2.50 (10366-5)

Dell Bestsellers

At your local bookstore or use this handy coupon for ordering:

INTRODUCING...

The Romance Magazine For The 1980's

Each exciting issue contains a full-length romance novel — the kind of first-love story we all dream about...

PLUS

other wonderful features such as a travelogue to the world's most romantic spots, advice about your romantic problems, a quiz to find the ideal mate for you and much, much more.

ROMANTIQUE: A complete novel of romance, plus a whole world of romantic features.

ROMANTIQUE: Wherever magazines are sold. Or write Romantique Magazine, Dept. C-1, 41 East 42nd Street, New York, N.Y. 10017

INTERNATIONALLY DISTRIBUTED BY
DELL DISTRIBUTING, INC.